HOCKEY HEART

A SINGLE DAD HOCKEY ROMANCE

THE 'SKATES AND SPARKS' SERIES

KATE WILDER

Copyright © 2024 by Kate Wilder

All rights reserved.

No part of this book may be reproduced in any form or by any electronic or mechanical means, including information storage and retrieval systems, without written permission from the author, except for the use of brief quotations in a book review.

To those who never stopped loving, even when it felt like the world was ending...

1

WORSER-ER

Sarah

"Bernard is the *worst*, Sarah! C'mon, he really said that to you?"

Kensy wasn't wrong, Bernard really was the worst, but it felt like a judgment on me when she said it like that. I mean, I'd chosen to go out with him, so what did that make me? Worser-er? Lamer-er?

"Oh, he said it alright," I put my glasses on and played awkwardly with the frame, stuttering in my best Bernard impression, "*I... I... Just don't think... Women should be... In... In politics. The... The... Hormones.*

"My God, that man!"

"Right!? I mean, who even thinks that, yet alone says it out loud to his date?"

"Uh huh," Kensy agreed, nodding and splashing a few drops of wine on my kitchen floor at the same time. "Good riddance!"

Okay, so Kensy, she's my best friend. I've known her for over four years now, ever since I joined Parkford Junior

Primary School. I hadn't meant to be a first-grade teacher, it certainly wasn't where I'd ever seen myself, but it wasn't the worst job I'd ever had either and, honestly, I'd been thankful for it at a time when I'd been... Well, let's just say, *lost,* for now.

Things hadn't been going too well for me in the year building up to all that, and that's a wild understatement. Coming back to my hometown as a complete emotional wreck was not what I'd seen in my future. Neither was living a small-town life in the suburban backwaters of America, alone and going nowhere, but that was how life had worked out. In truth, I was half-relieved. After all that trouble in California.

I'd needed something to keep me moving, not *forward* exactly, but at least not falling backward into a bleak black hole of miserable nothingness. So, I sleepwalked my way into taking my teaching exams. It was, at the very least, a welcome distraction and something to focus on that wasn't the nightmare that had put me there.

Then, before I knew it, I ended up subbing at Parkford, where I met Kensy. A neurotic, funny, and warm-hearted woman my own age, who wore improbably loud and out-of-fashion dresses (more often than not with 80s shoulder pads), laughed like an unhinged hyena, and shared my love of cheap gas station wine and both moaning or laughing about the lives we were living out.

Eventually, when Helen Potts had a full-blown seismic meltdown in class and left Parkford mid-term, I was there to slot neatly into her shadow. That had been four years ago. Somehow, the time had passed, and I felt like I'd never woken up.

Kensy, on the other hand, had already been there a year before I arrived and she came along when I desperately needed a friend. I hadn't told her about why I was back in Merryville at first - not about Jake, not about the immense swell of pain and all that agony I had brought back with me - but eventually it came out. You can't hide that much sadness for too long. It always finds a way to the surface.

Now, I was making it work. Getting on with life again. And I barely thought about it much more than that. I was just glad to have not sunk without a trace. To have narrowly avoided being swallowed up and then slowly and painfully digested in the cavernous stomach of events that had put me there.

But if Parkford Junior had saved me, it had also smothered me. I just couldn't see beyond it. If I'm honest, I had hoped that by that point in my life, someone would have come along, swept me off my feet, and saved me from the small life I'd willingly trapped myself in. But no one had come. And so there I was, fading away slowly with each passing day. Oh, and going on lame dates with guys like fucking *Bernard*.

I'd once aspired to more greatness than teaching kids how to not kill each other. Now, it gave me some safety, some security, all of which I needed. The kids also made me laugh more than they made me want to scream. It was only the parents who were the real downer.

Although I didn't say it out loud, the highlight of my week was mine and Kensy's Friday night wine and gossip nights. There wasn't a whole lot of gossip in truth, but we managed with what we had.

"...Into the last minute of the last game of the season and Hayden Raynor—The Hellraiser!—takes out Sampson with a HUGE hit to the boards..."

Kensy and I looked over to the television screen as we heard Hayden's name and I felt a familiar flutter of buttery excitement inside. 230lbs and 6' 8" of muscle, sex, and sweat on skates. He did something to me, that man, and I liked it. *God, what would it be like to have someone like that in your life? A raging protector, willing to destroy everything and everyone for you.*

"...And Sampson has dropped the gloves! They're going at it in the last minute here! The Hellraiser and the Stallion trading blows..."

"So, we're going, right?" Kensy said, her eyes still glued to the TV screen with mine. I smiled to myself at the thought and let those feelings flutter again.

"I mean look at that Kensy! We've got to!" I replied, as we watched Hayden now skating like a bloodied but victorious gladiator toward the penalty box. Every inch of him oozing masculine and rugged, raw power as the crowd went wild.

Hockey was a big thing in Merryville, and the Ice-Hawks had been the surprise hit of the league this year. Now it was the last game of the season, and that meant this coming Wednesday would be the end-of-season hockey charity ball. Normally, I wouldn't care too much about it, but not this year.

Kensy was actually going to get us in through her cousin, an events manager at the Glass House Arena. And then there was the *real* kicker... Hayden Raynor—all of that wild, rugged, violent man—would be up for grabs in this year's charity auction. *A night with the Hellraiser.* I sighed to myself dreamily.

"Hope you saved up some of that teacher's salary," Kensy said with a big grin on her face.

I sighed at the reality. "I could never afford him, Kensy. But my God! Could you imagine?"

It was true, I didn't have the kind of money it would take to live out my vivid fantasies of a date with the "Hellraiser". Still, it made me giddy to think about, and who knows? Maybe what Hayden was really looking for in his superstar life was a broken-hearted first-grade teacher, hurtling toward her thirties, in old clothes, living in a cheap one-bed rental in the bad end of town, with barely any life to speak of other than the teacher's quiz night every Wednesday.

"*Fuck*. Yes, Sarah! Yes, I can. And I will again when I get home tonight too!"

We laughed, but even so, I wanted to know what it would be like. Even just seeing him up close at the ball would be a thrill in itself.

The great thing about a celebrity crush is that it's a safe fantasy. They can be whoever who want them to be in your imagination, without ever having to face the stark reality. The perfect man. In all honesty, my fantasies of Hayden had become a bit of an obsession of late, but a girl needed some excitement, even if it was just something I dreamed up. A warm feeling rushed through my blood as my brain rewarded me with a tantalizing fantasy…

"Wow, that dress! Sarah, I'm so glad it was you who won the auction."

"I guess I don't scrub up so bad for a primary school teacher."

"Crazy idea babe, but how about we skip the restaurant and order room service instead?"

"You have a wicked look in your eye, Hayden. I like that."

"Well, you bought me, so I'm at your every command. Anything you want, Sarah. I'm all yours, all night…"

"Okay," I shrilled, shutting down my escalating daydream, turning off the television, and draining my glass in one swift movement. "It's a school night, so I'm calling an end to this and throwing you out."

"Fair enough," Kensy said as she hopped off the countertop. "See you tomorrow. Who knows? Hicks might even wear a new entertaining tie to cheer us all up."

I rolled my eyes with a smile. "Yeah. What a thrill."

It was a sparkling spring day as I pulled up to the school the next morning. The parking lot was full, as always. It was never smart to arrive late, or you ended up in the overflow, which was a good five-minute walk from the main doors of Parkford Junior. This morning I *was* late, because my fantasy-man, Hayden Raynor, had unexpectedly pulled back my shower curtain, climbed in, scrubbed me down oh-so tenderly and sexily with his giant soapy paws, then turned me against the wall and taken me like a wild beast until I had come like a howling steam train. These shower fantasies were really starting to get out of hand, and they had only increased in intensity now that the hockey ball was coming up.

"Those goddamn parents taking up the teaching spots. Someone should do something about it," John Princeton huffed from behind me, already out of breath.

"Maybe we should set their cars on fire before we go in, as a warning," I joked.

John didn't get the joke and squinted at me, trying to tell if I'd gone over the edge and was actually about to descend into violence and disorder. *Yes! The revolution was here and we were taking our parking spaces back!*

"You going to the teacher quiz tomorrow night?" He asked.

"Nope," I told him with a delighted smile on my face. "Me and Kensy are hitting up the hockey ball."

"Oh, very nice!"

"I plan on buying myself a hockey player and then living the high life, John."

"Sure you will. Hey, and then you can bring them to the quiz! We need someone who's good for the sports round."

A pang of annoyance seared through my bubble of excitement, popping it painfully with the stark reality that what I'd said would never actually happen. Growing up, I'd always believed that I'd get whisked away by some movie star, pop star, maybe a cowboy, or a German gymnast (okay, maybe that's just me. But I developed a strange and very unhealthy fixation with Johan Greiger after the 2020 Olympics). Even after I'd lowered my expectations to settle for a stage actor, author, pilot, or a plumber (hey, it's a practical choice and they're literally never out of work, okay?), it still turned out no one was coming to save me.

But that's not really love, is it? They're just fantasies. Now *those* I had in abundance, although they had seemed to dim recently. Except for perhaps one... Hayden.

2

SILVER STUD

Hayden

"Do you think it's cute?"

I frowned back at the eager-eyed brunette. Her pink tongue pushed out luridly, showing off the silver stud that glistened like a robot pearl on a pink oyster. A sharp jolt of excitement ran through me, seeing that wet organ dripping in front of my eyes. *The things I could do with that mouth...*

As she saw my eyes and thoughts darken, the brunette's smile quickly turned into a giggle, and she fluttered her lashes at me. I glanced down to take in the two long and smooth tan legs that ran all the way up and under her short loose dress.

"Sure, it's cute, but what does it feel like?" I asked, as my gaze returned to meet hers.

The brunette lowered her eyes at me seductively, took my hand, and then lifted it up to her mouth, before slipping her plump alluring lips over my thumb. A ripple of excitement shook through me as her soft lips closed over my delighted digit.

"Feels pretty good," I told her, smiling and circling the piercing with my thumb.

"Wub Wuh," she agreed.

"Why would you..." I started to say, but I didn't have the heart to ruin her moment, "...Anyway, yeah, it's cute." I had to bellow at her over the thump of the music to make her hear me.

Kelly... Katie... *What was her name?* ...The brunette slipped my glistening thumb from her mouth, letting her lips roll slowly right over it. Then she returned my hand to me and went back to busily pulling cutesy faces and taking selfies.

As I watched her happily tapping on her phone, it felt like there were three of us together, and it was me who was the third wheel. Not that I minded so much. Being a wingman for my wingman wasn't my first choice tonight. We'd just wrapped up the end of a long season and all I felt was aching tiredness and a sharp, dull pain around my eye socket, right where I'd taken a fist from Sampson in the last game. My own fist was still swollen, and I pressed it up against the beer bottle in my hand, looking for a blissful soothing sensation, but finding it disappointingly warm.

Christ, why was it so damn loud in here, anyway? The music—if you could call it that—was a never-ending, pounding death march. I'd give anything to be home, sipping on a cold beer in my hot tub, and listening to Cindi Lauper. Instead, I'm at the most pink bar I've ever seen in my life, sipping a warm beer on a giant fucking bean bag, and watching... Kristen? Kirsty? Kayley? ...Well, *whatever her name was*, take selfies.

Look, I mean, I'm a big guy, and most girls cream themselves over the fact that I'm 6' 8" of glistening raw muscle, looking like some kind of Viking warlord who's about to raze their hometown, take away their repressed women-folk, and then make them raise huge Viking babies. My reputation doesn't do me any harm either, but I really wasn't in the mood for it tonight. To be honest, I hadn't been in the mood for it for much longer than tonight.

Not that I had a choice, though. See, the big problem with being a hockey player—or, at least *one* of the big problems—is you're basically in a dysfunctional family with twenty-three huge, unpredictable, and often violent brothers. If you think that sounds hectic, you don't even know the half of it. Especially when you're out on the road. Being captain of the Ice-Hawks also means I end up being the dad figure more often than I'd like. Randall needed me tonight to distract—*Damn! What the hell was it? Kimmy? Kasey?*—while he put the moves on her friend, Georgia, some bigshot influencer he'd had his eye on since they became Instabuddies a few weeks back. I figured I was trapped there for another half hour at least.

"Oh my god! Look!" the tongue-pierced brunette screeched, suddenly thrusting her phone at my face.

"My friend Chelsea is at the Cinnamon Lounge with Sean LeBlanc. We should do a double date!"

"I don't date," I growled back.

She glowered at me. That made me feel good.

"Well, can I get a selfie for my gram?"

I sighed at her. This was getting exhausting. These puck bunnies seemed to get more annoying every year. And why did they all talk like that? Like they were children who really wanted a pony or something.

"Pretty pleeeease," she said brightly, doing some odd wide-eyed pose that was supposed to be adorable but just pissed me off.

"Fine," I huffed back.

"Yay! Let me sit on your knee and take it."

Before I'd even had a chance to think, she was on me, holding out her phone and throwing up her fingers in the now-standard international selfie sign. Why did her phone have pink bunny ears on it? Ugh, I hated this.

The brunette lingered on my thigh and giggled playfully.

"That feels nice, doesn't it?"

Someone had clearly forgotten to put panties on today, I thought, as I also wondered how hard it was going to be to get up and off this giant bean bag later.

I rolled my eyes, and we both glanced over at Randall and Georgia, who were lost in their own gooey world, canoodling and cooing at each other across from us.

Babe, you just get it, don't you?
I really do!
God, you're so hot, look at you.
I really am!

I'd heard it all before, but it looked promising that things might wrap up even earlier than I had hoped for. My date turned her eyes back from the canoodling and looked at me with a hopeful and seductive smile, wondering if we might end up doing the same. My tired expression told her exactly how likely that was. Finally, and mercifully, she went back to clicking on her phone. Still didn't get off my thigh, though.

And it was true. *I didn't date.* I took another swig of my warm beer and grimaced. It tasted like piss.

"Hayden Raynor!" Some blonde girl was suddenly hollering at me, "Come party with us tonight!"

"Not tonight, thanks though."

"Aww, really?"

That damn voice again. Who even started that? I briefly

imagined a world where John O'Connor had to go back in time to stop the first person who did it from existing, saving us all from this hell. Across from us, Randall and Georgie had broken off their eye-fucking and had started to get up.

"Hayden," Randall yelled over the thumping music from hell, "I think we're gonna head out."

The smile on his face told me what that meant. *Thank God for that.*

"Cool man, I gotta be heading too."

I looked down at *Kermit? Krispy?* But she was lost in her phone, contorting another faux innocent smile at the camera. Was she happy being like this? Were any of us happy being like this?

I considered my options, then with minimal grace, rolled over onto the floor like a seal in order to escape the bean bag of embarrassment.

3

EVERYTHING MUST GO

Sarah

Waking up that Wednesday morning, I found myself fizzing with a wild energy. Even a quick steamy fantasy shower session with Hayden hadn't taken the edge off. I couldn't think straight. My head was scrambled only with rich half-fantasies of the evening that lay ahead.

Wednesday was my half-day at Parkford and I spent that whole morning distracted and on edge. There was an insistent nagging going on inside me that I couldn't seem to dampen, making me feel manic, jumpy, and unpredictable.

When those ridiculous ideas had first flooded into my head, I should have stopped them right there and then, but in my ever-building frenzy, I already knew I was about to do something stupid and out of character, and I was helpless to resist.

I found myself driving back to my apartment after lunch, filling a large cardboard box, then heading over to the East side, unable to stop myself hurtling toward what I already knew was certain disaster.

What the hell are you doing, Sarah? This was not me. Maybe I was tired of being *me*, though. Safe Sarah, with her quiet job and her lonely apartment. Well, for once, to hell with all that. I turned off my rational brain, despite its screeching protests, and in a daze, I pulled my car into the dealership and walked up to the sleek glass doors.

"Hi there! What can we do for you today? Looking to buy, sell, trade up?"

I hated salesman-ship and wanted to get this over as quickly as possible. Before I had a chance to reclaim my thoughts and change my mind.

"How much would I get for that?" I said, pointing out of the glass windows to my red Chevy Trax. A pang of instant regret rose up at how flippantly I was offering up my beloved car for this madness. It had been named Toto on its first girls' road trip down to New Orleans years ago and I truly loved that car. It was a dear old friend, and we'd had some real scrapes and adventures over the years.

"Well, let's go take a look!" said the annoyingly beaming man in his suit.

Half an hour later, I walked out of the dealership with the cardboard box of belongings from the trunk, a cheque for $5,000, and tried my best not to think about Toto watching me leave her behind.

Having made one ridiculous leap, I now had an even more powerful resolve to see this through. I'd already started, so there was no going back now, or else what was the point? Walking across the street to the dusty-looking pawn shop, I entered with the box of the most precious items I'd gathered throughout my life.

"Hey there!" The pawn shop owner yelped, seeming surprised at encountering another person as I stepped out of the sun and into the musty and gloomy shop. Each wall of the store was stacked with a jumble of cabinets that held a mismatch of people's property that they had chosen—or more likely been forced to by circumstance—to turn into money instead.

As it turned out, the pawnbroker wasn't all that interested in the most valuable things in my life. A lamp from Paris, a signed copy of Kitchen Confidential, an old laptop that only worked if it stayed plugged in, a few not-so-rare records.

"I can give you $100 for the lot."

"Really? I was hoping for more."

He looked at me ruefully, lifting his hands to say, *it's all I can do*. As he saw the disappointment written across my face, he glanced down.

"If you really need the money, how about this?"

I looked down to where his eyes were fixed with a sinking feeling. I already knew what he had spied. That ring on my finger had been my grandma's, the only thing I had left of her after she died six years back. I hadn't taken it off, even once, since.

"Nice diamond, probably worth $2,000."

"$3,000," I said, surprising myself with the words from my mouth.

"Hmm, $2,200, okay?"

"Three," I said flatly. He took a look at my expression and could see this was no longer a negotiation.

"Can't do it," he finally said.

"Okay, just the other stuff, then."

We settled up, and I went to leave, a measly $100 richer, when he spoke up again.

"$2,800 *and* I'll let you buy it back for the same price for seven days. After that, I sell it."

I stumbled out of the pawnbroker in a daze. I probably

should have felt deflated and annoyed at my losses, but there's some odd mystic power that money seems to hold, making me instead feel a warm glow of achievement. In less than an hour, I had nearly eight thousand bucks. With the four I already had in my savings, that gave me a hefty twelve grand.

The idea stirred up a nice fuzzy feeling inside. I was fairly sure that it wasn't anywhere near enough to buy a star hockey player for the night, but still, I could at least go get my ring back and pick up another cheaper car. I had a painful pang of annoyance at giving away my Parisian lamp though for, what, ten bucks at best? I guess maybe I could buy that back, too.

It was madness, and I knew I'd feel ashamed about it later, but it would all be okay. Unless it wasn't. But then I would be out with Hayden *fucking* Raynor. A burst of excitement rushed through me at the thought, making me unexpectedly blush. *Christ, get it together Sarah!*

Having traded up the most valuable things in my life just for the chance to put a bid on a hockey player, I had five hours left to swing by the bank, deposit both the check and cash, then get myself ready for tonight. With an unexpected spring in my step, I set off.

4

FLETCH, THE SON OF A BITCH

Hayden

"You got to be kidding, Fletch?"

"Hayden, you just stand up there, let them throw money at you, go for dinner, play nice, and then it's all done."

I stared dumbly at him.

"Hayden, it's for kids with cancer, for the love of God!"

I sighed heavily. I couldn't say no, but honestly, standing up on that stage being gawped at and then sold struck me as something we were meant to have gotten past by now. At least I'd already told Joyce, so that was one less thing to worry about.

"Not sure this'll help," I told Fletch, pointing at the black eye that was still throbbing on my face.

"It might actually make you *more* appealing," Fletch beamed back. "Everyone likes a bad boy."

Goddamnit. It'd be nice if just for one second someone saw me as something other than a raging bull. Then again, that was how I made my living. It's how I protected *us*. And one day, it would eventually all be over.

I looked down at my red knuckles and thought about Sampson. What the heck was the point of fighting with one minute left of the season, anyway? I wouldn't have minded so much, but things seemed to take longer to heal these days. Next thing I would start getting slow, then I'd start losing the fights, missing the bodychecks, and then it really would all be over. That didn't annoy me so much, I was looking forward to it. Well, maybe that's not *entirely* true. I had no idea what would come next, what life without hockey would look like, and a big part of me found that absolutely terrifying. It also reminded me with a shudder that I really had to solve this thing with Cara before then, before it could ruin me, ruin *us*.

Just then Solly came into the office, rambling and looking like he'd seen a ghost.

"Fletch, I can't do it! Maria, she's mad as hell, says it's a deal-breaker if I let it happen. Please Fletch, you gotta..."

"Solly...," Fletch began, shaking his head at the panic-filled left winger in front of him.

He was enjoying this, I thought. Then I realized I was too.

"...It's contractual. My hands are tied. You just gotta go out there, make some money for charity, and have a nice dinner. That's it."

"You try telling Maria that! She's furious Fletch. You should've heard her, throwing things at me, threatening to kick me out."

For a second, Fletch smiled dryly, then it disappeared in a flash before Solly could notice it.

Fletch arranged all our promotional events, sponsorships, and everything on the commercial side, and he was a persuasive son of a bitch. Or, honestly, just a son of a bitch most of the time. I'd also noticed him talking to Maria whenever she came along to events with Solly, and I had a sense that there was something between them. No wonder he was enjoying this.

I could also see that Solly was overboard, swimming in deep waters with fins circling around him, panicking and looking for something, *anything*, to cling onto to save him. I swiftly made my exit before he tried to grab onto me as his lifeline. I might be the toughest guy on the ice, but even I couldn't handle the fury of Maria Ricek when she got going.

"Later guys, I'm already late."

"See you tonight," Fletch called after me, "Oh, and dress nice, would ya!" he added as I swept through the doorway.

I turned the corner in the hallway and ran straight into Dan Janek.

"Hellmaster," he said in a sinister tone, with an odd grin.

"Hell-*raiser*," I corrected him.

Dan had come into the team this season from some small village in Finland, and the guy spoke a type of English that was almost, but never quite, right. Some guys prayed before the game, instead Dan roared like he was in a black metal band. It was an interesting contrast. Hell of a goaltender too.

"If you're going to see Fletch to try and get out of tonight, I'd forget it. Solly is in there doing his best right now and getting nowhere."

"Ah, no. I want to be buyed up by some rich American lady, babies in the backroom."

"Babies in the *what* now?"

And with that, Dan nodded in agreement and walked off with a wide grin, as if our conversation had come to a natural and pleasing conclusion.

All I wanted to do in the world was to go sit on a beach and sleep for the next six weeks. This season had felt like it had gone on forever and my body had taken an absolute battering. When you get a reputation like mine, everyone wants to take down the king, and it gets pretty exhausting dealing with that every game night.

The last thing I needed was to play nice over dinner with some rich man's wife who wanted to get me into a hotel room so she could tell all her rich wife friends about it.

I'd just play it like always. If they wanted the *Hellraiser*, then that's what they'd get, and there would be no apologies for it. Outside, I climbed into my truck and started the ignition, the stereo flashing into life and *Total Eclipse of The Heart* blasting out of the speakers... God, I *loved* this song! I took a quick look around for any prying eyes, before collapsing my head back against the seat and joining in loudly.

My hollering was stopped in its tracks as the music muted and changed into a ringtone. Annoyed, I looked at the caller's name on the truck's dashboard and winced. Cara was not who I wanted to talk to right now. I *really* had to figure out what to do about her, but I had no idea what that would be yet. Instead of hanging up, I just let it dial out until the music came roaring back.

5

THE BID

Sarah

"OH MY GOOODDDD! Can you believe tonight is happening!?" Kensy hollered down the phone as I put her on speaker so I could finish my make-up while we chatted.

"I know!" I said, my stomach fluttering nervously in response to her outburst of excitement, "Oh, erm, Kensy, could you maybe pick me up? I, sort of... Well, I sold my car."

"What, Toto? No! Not because..."

"Yeah. You don't have to tell me. I already feel stupid and embarrassed enough about it. But, hey, I can get another car, right?"

"Er... Sure you will, unless you make babies with that barbarian," she laughed down the line.

"Yeah, I'm not sure how much Hayden Raynor a few thousand bucks would get me. Maybe there's a cheaper option? Perhaps that Czech one with the massive eyebrows?"

"Voracek! You'd have to pay *me* to go out with *him*... Dan Janek isn't so bad, though."

"The goaltender! You serious?"

"Good with his hands," Kensy said dreamily.

"Haha, okay. I'll be ready in like an hour."

"You're crazy Sarah. I love you. See you in an hour!"

Kensy arrived wearing a flowing black dress covered in overlapping triangles in neon pink, purple, and lemon lines. We made for an odd couple with me in my simple midnight-blue cocktail dress, but I was proud of her for sticking to her style and not even trying to dress appropriately for the occasion. For me, however, I was still trying to find my way by desperately trying to look like everyone else, trying to give the impression that I fitted in and felt like a normal person inside. Not standing out seemed like all I could do to be safe.

When we arrived, there was valet parking, but we'd skipped it and instead parked Kensy's Prius at the far end of the car park, in order not to embarrass ourselves.

It felt good as we walked up to the Glass House with the rest of the glamorous crowd. With the flashing cameras and the carpet rolled out, it was like we were really a part of that elite set, even if only for a short-lived moment.

"Oh look! That's Randall Jackson with Georgia Moss," Kensy said in a hushed voice, her eyes leading the way as we approached the carpet. A flash of photographer's lights boomed around us like fireworks exploding. Kensy's curtsy in front of the camera crowd got a less fanatical reaction with one tepid camera flash that left us laughing at each other.

Inside, we both scooped a glass of champagne from a

passing tray and watched the gaggle of people in expensive clothes having loud and jovial conversations. We were like ghosts in that room. No one even looked twice at us, let alone spoke to us. I was thankful when, finally, the lights dimmed for the start of the auction, my anxiety and feeling of imposter syndrome having started to climb toward dangerous levels. I really didn't want to stand there and be ignored all night.

We all looked toward the stage as the presenter walked out. An impossibly smooth-skinned older man, with hair that was too black to be untreated, I couldn't help but see him as entirely gray underneath.

"Oh, I know him! He was on that show... Blue Bloods or SVU or something..." Kensy told me.

"Daniel Day-Lewis was busy tonight, so instead they got the man who taught him everything he knows..." the man began, flashing an impeccable white smile at us all, then working his way through an introduction that mostly focused on how we should all be giving away as much of our money as possible. The wives and younger men in the room seemed delighted with this, while the older crowd looked dryly and solemnly ahead, sensing their wallets were in danger.

"Onto our first auction item of the night, please raise your checkbooks for... Solly Ricek!"

Solly walked out uncomfortably to a round of applause that made my heart beat faster. A nervous expression stretched across his pale face. Looking to my right, I saw a gorgeous woman standing in an open-backed dress by the stage. Her slim tan arms were crossed, glaring directly at him. Solly tried to soften her glare with a small pleading smile, but seeing him flash his teeth at her only seemed to make her even more mad.

I nudged Kensy and nodded my head toward the woman.

"Uh-oh, Solly's getting in trouble," she said, her expression one of amused delight.

"So. Who's going to start us off?" The announcer boomed from the stage.

"Two bucks!" someone yelled out to a ripple of laughter.

"Fifty!"

"Two hundred!" A plump, bespectacled older lady in a cardigan near us shouted enthusiastically.

"Five hundred." The open-backed goddess said flatly, still staring furiously at poor Solly.

"A thousand." The woman in the cardigan yelled. She was all riled up now, like she was watching her horse winning the Kentucky Derby. Hopping from foot to foot, all sweaty and buzzed up on the excitement.

"Two." the scorned woman responded.

"Five!" came the immediate response from next to us. *God, she was in it to win it*, I thought. This was going to be interesting.

The Goddess paused, wavered a moment, then found whatever resolve she needed and plowed ahead.

"Six."

"Seven!"

"Eight."

"Ten! Ten thousand!" The Cardigan was jumping with excitement now, her face red and flushed with the rush. On the stage, Solly gulped nervously.

"Twelve."

"Fifteen!"

The Goddess threw a dirty look over her shoulder at the Cardigan, but the Cardigan was only looking at Solly.

"Twenty," she said, emotionless.

"Twenty-five!"

"Thirty."

"Fifty!"

The Goddess balked at this. The Cardigan wasn't going to stop. There must be a limit? Some point where the scales went over. But, looking at her, it didn't seem that way. She was unrelenting in the pursuit of her prize.

"Fifty-one," the Goddess said weakly. She was reaching a point that she wasn't prepared for.

"One hundred!"

There was a gasp from the crowd and all eyes were now turned to the Cardigan, who was bouncing in glee, before they turned back to the glaring Goddess who looked stunned, and then, after swaying for a moment, she sat down.

"SOLD! For... Ladies and gentlemen... ONE HUNDRED THOUSAND DOLLARS! Give it up for Solly Ricek, and..." The announcer stretched his hand out toward the Cardigan.

"Beth Gibson!" She yelled back.

"Give it up for Solly Ricek and his very generous date for the evening, Beth Gibson!"

Solly was sweating profusely on the stage now, his eyes darting from the audience to the scowling terror that was sitting by the stage trying to murder him with her eyes.

"Oh, I know her!" Kensy said in my ear, nodding at the Cardigan, "She's the one who got divorced from that tech billionaire, it was in all the gossip news, took him for everything she could get."

"Well, now she's got Solly Ricek too," I said back, still shocked at what we'd just witnessed.

"Poor Solly, she's going to eat him alive," said Kensy, and I nodded in agreement before we both looked back over at the seething brunette. Someone came to put a reassuring hand on her shoulder, and she batted it away with a vicious swipe.

"Next up... Mister Safe Hands... The man you want between your pipes," a few chuckles came from the now enraptured and engaged crowd, "give it up for Dan Janek!"

"Yes!" Kensy screeched, before yelling out, "Three hundred and twenty-seven dollars!"

The presenter looked a little annoyed that his announcement to start the bidding had been taken away from him, but he rolled past it.

"An opening bid already... Three hundred dollars!"

"And twenty-seven!" Kensy yelled back, but he ignored her as the other bids started coming in.

"Four hundred... Five... Six... One thousand..."

I looked at Kensy and she shrugged.

"I went all in, worth a shot."

Dan Janek pulled in a decent twenty-eight thousand dollars while Kensy glowered as a cheerful middle-aged mom skipped over to the stage to claim her prize.

"Ugh, she wouldn't know what to do with him."

"Probably put him on babysitting duty for the night," I said, trying to lighten the mood.

But there was an anxious feeling in my stomach that I was trying to ignore, and it was growing rapidly. Then it was quickly joined by my heart thumping like thunder in my chest as I noticed a shadow looming on the side of the stage.

"Here we go! Our next item, the man with the iron fists, and ladies, it's not just his fists that are rock hard..." the announcer winked to an equal scattering of chuckles and groans. But I didn't laugh or groan. I couldn't. My hands were sweaty and my mouth wouldn't stop awkwardly twitching.

Kensy turned to me and saw my face. "You okay, Sarah?"

"Uh-huh," I managed to mutter back, swallowing down a gulp as the man from all of my recent fantasies stepped out in real life before me onto the stage.

"...Hayden, *The Hellraiser*, Raynor!"

Kensy howled along with the crowd, but I was detached from it all, my eyes feasting eagerly on his frame. His roguish brown hair and dark stubble, his huge chest underneath a stretched white t-shirt that looked like it might tear open with just a flex of one of his muscles. He looked even bigger in person than I had expected.

"So then, who wants a night with the *Hellraiser*?"

There was a wild ripple of excited cheers, but I was entirely removed from it, fixated only on Hayden beaming from the stage at all the attention that was being given to him. For a second, his head passed over the clapping hands and it seemed like he was looking right at me. A tremble ran through me before I noticed Kensy tugging on my arm.

"Sarah? You ready to get your bid in?"

She was looking at me wide-eyed, all caught up in the excitement and, suddenly, I was pulled back down to earth, back to the room and the announcer's voice booming around us.

"Two thousand! Three thousand. Four. Five..."

"Sarah! Put your hand up!"

Half-dazed, I looked to the stage. The lights seemed lurid and bright. I felt sick.

"Over here!" Kensy shouted at the stage and lifted my arm.

"Eight thousand!" the announcer bellowed our way as my arm fell back down.

"Nine! Ten!"

I snapped back into action. This was the moment I'd

waited for, but I couldn't enjoy it. I was a ball of stress. My arm went up.

"Eleven!"

"Twelve," the announcer pointed to the other side of the room, "Thirteen... Fourteen... FIFTEEN THOUSAND... Sixteen..."

My chance had gone and everything faded. Standing in that room with all those rich and glamorous people, I suddenly just felt flat and alone. What had I expected would happen? I mean, *really*?

"...Twenty-five, ladies and gentlemen! Thirty! Thirty-five!"

I could sense Kensy looking at me pitifully from my side. All I wanted to do was to leave immediately and maybe have a quiet cry alone outside. *Ridiculous Sarah, this was nothing but a childish fantasy.* Hayden Raynor? *Who were you kidding anyway?*

A rasping voice from behind us broke me out of my spell.

"Keep bidding."

I turned to see a well-dressed man in a black tie and suit, his blue eyes fixed on me.

"Huh? I don't... I can't..."

"Please. I'll comp you."

"What? I don't understand," I stuttered back.

The man flashed a look across the room, toward a young blonde woman in a sequin dress that I thought made her look like a disco ball crossed with a mermaid.

"My fiance. I can't let her win *him*."

He had a pained expression, one that only someone who is truly desperate knows how to pull.

"*Please*," he insisted again.

The disco mermaid flung her hand in the air and the girls around her squealed with delight.

"FIFTY THOUSAND DOLLARS!"

I watched the man for a moment longer, making sure he was absolutely serious, then I turned back to the stage and flung my arm up.

"Fifty-five!"

The fiance's hand went up again, "Sixty!"

Then the announcer's eyes came back my way, and I did the same, "Sixty-five!"

"How much?" I whispered over my shoulder.

"What?" He replied.

"How MUCH?"

"Just keep going," he insisted.

I flung my hand up again, the fiance immediately doing the same, "Seventy-five! Eighty!"

We were the only two playing the game now.

"Eighty-five! Ninety! Ninety-five!"

She wavered and scowled over at me, but I only looked ahead.

Then, as if in a dream, it was all over. I couldn't understand what had happened exactly, until I heard Kensy's voice screaming at me, "You won! You won!"

I looked down at my hands and saw they were shaking. Then I turned back to where the man had been standing. He was gone. My heart raced.

"Kensy, hold my drink!" I said frantically, and then I was running through the crowd.

6

A MERMAID & A DISASTER

Sarah

No, no, no. This can't be happening!

I rampaged through the room, desperately looking for him. I'd just won a date. My dumb, unattainable fantasy had come true, and now it had slipped away with a sequined girl into the night, my dreams going with it.

The table with his fiance was now deserted. He wasn't at the bar or at the stage, or any of the other tables. *What did he even look like, exactly?* I'd only glimpsed him for a moment over my shoulder. Kensy reached my side, panting, and between breaths, she pointed to a door leading outside.

Bursting out into the parking lot, I looked around frantically. Then, out of the corner of my eye, I saw a flash of mermaid heading into the darkness. Narrowing my eyes with purpose, I scurried toward those sequins uncomfortably, cursing my heels.

"I don't see why we have to leave now. You're embarrassing me!" The mermaid was protesting to the man who held my hopes in his wallet.

"Hey!" I yelled, when I was close enough for him to hear.

They both turned around and stared at me. He looked as uncomfortable as my feet were in that moment and my eyes blazed at him.

The mermaid looked at him and asked, "Who's that?"

"Oh, er," he dallied, searching for something reasonable to say, "She's the new... Secretary."

The mermaid looked at me unimpressed. When I didn't say anything, she blurted out rudely, "Well, what do you want?"

Just at that moment, a shriek rang out behind me.

"Laaannaa! Where did you go?"

"Christiieeeee," the mermaid bawled back, "Oh my god, Edward says we have to go!"

I saw my chance as the girls went to embrace each other and quickly approached him. "You'd better write that check right now, or I'm about to tell that girl everything that happened in there."

The man - the one I'd just found out was called Edward - gulped, considered his options, and realizing he didn't have any, pulled out his checkbook.

"How much are you short?"

"Eighty-three thousand dollars!"

His eyes looked like they were about to pop out of his head.

"Edward!" the mermaid howled, "Let's stay for just one more!"

"Get on with it," I growled at him under my breath.

"Okay, just one!" He called back, and then he scrawled out the numbers on his checkbook.

"You should be thanking me," he hissed as he thrust the paper into my outstretched palm.

In return, I threw him a look that told him exactly what I

thought to that, before I turned on my heels to go and claim my rightful prize. Striding back into the ball, Kensy was by the doors, looking for me.

"There you are! Did you get him!?"

I nodded, looking down at the check in my hands like it was a golden ticket. In a funny kind of way, I guess it was. Was this really happening?

"Then let's go get him!"

It only hit me properly then. By *him,* she meant Hayden Raynor. I actually had a *date* with *Hayden Raynor*!

We found the auctioneer's assistant by the stage, looking annoyed.

"There you are! You're meant to come straight up to the stage."

Kensy chimed in, "Bathroom break. I have a weak bladder. Is that a problem?"

He stared back at her uncomfortably, and then sighed painfully.

"Check?"

"Oh, actually two checks!"

After I handed them to him, he seemed a lot more relaxed. "Well, Mrs. Mitchell…"

"Miss!" I corrected him, still in disbelief.

"Okay, *Miss* Mitchell. Just go through those doors and enjoy your evening."

Kensy was hopping and clapping her hands together next to me. We hugged excitedly, before I turned in a daze and left her to go and meet my destiny.

Through the double doors, he was already there, waiting. For a moment I could hardly breathe as I looked up at him, actually standing in front of me, waiting for his date with *me*.

"Hi Hayden," I said, with shy velvet on my tongue.

"Yeah. Hi." He barely took a glance at me.

"Nice shirt," I offered.

It wasn't really a nice shirt, it was just a white t-shirt. But I suppose what I really meant was *love that torso on you*. Maybe he'd throw me a compliment back, something I could really savor for weeks - or even months - afterward, and then we'd smile and go on our date.

"Huh? Okay." He grunted, looking down at the cotton that covered the ripple of muscles below.

He looked back up at me dumbly, before mumbling flatly, "I guess let's go eat or something."

"I'd like that," I gushed back at him.

Should I slide my arm into his? Take his hand?

He turned and walked away from me, so I ended up just trotting behind him, awkwardly trying to keep up with his impossibly long strides in my five-inch heels.

As we headed toward the end of the corridor, there was a man waiting for us. Hayden nodded at him as we approached, him striding, me trotting.

"So, Fletch, am I supposed to drive or..."

"No, there's a limo waiting for you outside," the man said. To which Hayden visibly rolled his eyes, before he turned his giant head back to me.

"After you, Sandra."

"Sarah," I corrected him.

"Sure."

I looked up at him, and when he didn't bother to look back, I just followed his outstretched arm out the back of the building.

The ride was a short one, but the silence made it feel like forever. Hayden stared glumly out the limo window while I smoothed out my dress and tried not to blush the whole way. This was my chance to go out on a date with the great Hayden Raynor. I couldn't waste it.

"Do you know the place we're going to?" I asked.

"Nope." He said, still staring out of the window, his chin resting along one big meaty fist, looking bored.

I felt a sharp pang of disappointment and embarrassment. I'd let myself get carried away. Of *course*, I wasn't what he had hoped for, or would ever be interested in. I had to try, though. Once we broke the ice, surely we could have *some* fun. Maybe I just needed to get on his level.

"Hey, I saw you take down that Sampson guy in the last game. You were brilliant!"

"You were there?" He grunted back.

"No. I mean, I saw it on TV."

"Oh." was his one-word response to this.

Damnit, why wasn't I there? Because tickets were going for over three hundred bucks was why!

"Think the team have got a chance next year?"

"A chance for... *what*?"

"Y'know, the Championship!"

He grunted and shrugged.

This was not going how I had hoped, but I wasn't ready to give up and spied the ice bucket next to us.

"Ooh, champagne! Shall we be naughty and have a glass?"

"You go for it," he waved his hand at me.

With nothing else for it, I poured myself a glug into a long-stemmed glass and we sat quietly for the rest of the drive while I sipped slowly on the fizzing glass of bubbles. In truth, it tasted as sweet and bad as gas station sparkling wine, and I would know.

Things got worse at the restaurant. Hayden didn't pull my seat out for me, didn't ask me what I liked on the menu, or even if I'd like a drink. When the waiter first approached us and asked if we'd like to order drinks or starters, he just said, "Beer and chicken wings."

"Oh, we don't do chicken wings here. Perhaps I could recommend the duck confit?"

"You don't do wings?" He asked incredulously.

"Um, okay. Let me ask the chef and we'll see what we can do."

Hayden turned back to the menu while the waiter looked nervously at him.

"And for the lady?"

"Oh, a glass of red, please."

"Okay, which one?"

"Erm, whatever's a good one, but not too expensive, just, y'know, a normal one."

I sounded stupid and flustered and I would have been annoyed with myself if Hayden had even noticed.

"Okay, I'll come back for your food order when you've had a chance to look at the menu," our waiter said, flashing a nervous glance at Hayden who was now aggressively chewing the nails on one of his massive paws and still pretending to read the menu.

I wondered for a moment if he could even read. What if he was just insecure and being like this because he couldn't? He'd never even had to with being a hockey player. I could help him and bring him out of his shell and turn his life around. Imagine the world of menus and other foods that would open up to him!

"What's potato dolphins?" He asked without looking at the waiter, who had nearly made his escape.

"Um, potato dauphinoise? It's a sauteed potato in a rich creamy bechamel sauce that our chef prepares in a very special..."

"Yeah. That. And the wings."

"If we *can* do them, how many of those would you want?"

"Like, ten pounds I guess."

"Ten pounds! That's quite a lot of..."

"Uhh, I know my wings. That's what, forty wings? Forty is good."

The waiter stood staring at Hayden with hatred burning in his eyes.

"I'll just have the duck confit, thank you," I said, handing my menu back to the waiter, hoping that taking his earlier recommendation might oddly smooth things over.

"Very good," the waiter said, before fleeing. I wondered how that conversation in the kitchen would go.

"Would you really eat forty wings?" I asked after a moments more silence, trying to sound interested.

"Uh huh," Hayden said, still not looking up from the menu.

"Gee, lotta wings! Well... What do you do when you're not playing hockey?"

"Eat wings. Drink beer. Drive around I guess."

"Oh. Well, do you have family here?"

He flinched at this and then decided not to answer me.

"I'm going to use the bathroom," I finally told him, receiving no response. I really wanted to kick him under the table and tell him to have some manners, but I don't think he would've noticed that either.

In the bathroom, I looked at my miserable face. I was wearing my cutest dress, my make-up delicately conjured to show off my nice eyes and mouth. My long brown hair pressed, straightened, and then lightly curled to perfection. On my neck was a soft and delightful hint of my favorite French perfume that was down to the last couple of drops in the bottle. Not to mention all that had gone on under that dress. All this, and the man couldn't even look at me. Was I that bad? That unworthy? I felt those old and strong feelings of rejection and torment return. The same ones that I'd spent the last five years trying to lock into a box I would never have to open again. Yet, there they were, rising again to mock me.

I took a long breath and gave myself a steely look. *You get back out there and you try harder damnit! This isn't over yet.*

7

A DISASTER, PART 2

Hayden

Maybe I scared her off enough to call it quits. There was something weird about her. Not *bad* weird, just *different* weird. They're usually all giggly and say dumb things like, "Oh, you're *so* big, I bet it's massive," or "I work out. You wanna see how tight it all is."

A lot of the other guys love that stuff. Randall Jackson, for one. He couldn't get enough of it. Not me, though. Not anymore. Not since Cara. I closed my eyes, trying to put Cara out of my head. This one though, Sandra? Shiela? Deborah? Christ, whatever she was called... She just seemed kinda... Normal. Cute, in an odd way, too. I'd tried not to show her any interest - always a bad idea when you're a pro hockey bad-boy - but those were truly beautiful lips, and the soft creamy roll of her neck, and the way she spoke like she wasn't in some Tik-Tok video... *Oh hell, she was coming back...* Nice legs, even in that dress that looked like it came straight out of the sale section at Nordstrom Rack. Who was this woman?

Our eyes briefly connected as she arrived back at the table, and I couldn't not look dreamily for a moment into those vibrant green opals. Fortunately, our uptight waiter returned to stop me falling right into them.

"Your wings, sir. And a beer."

"Bring another beer. I'll finish this one in the time it takes you to get it. Actually, make it two."

He stared at me like I was an animal. Well, that's what I wanted them all to think, so to hell with it.

"Right you are, sir. Madame, your wine."

She was a *madame* type. The kind you pulled the seat out for her to sit down, not because you *had* to, but because she *should* be treated like a lady. Instead, I picked up a wing as she hovered at the table, until she finally took the hint and sat herself down.

"How are the wings?"

That voice was like soft velvet. Smart and controlled. Not like the loud and dumb-sounding blah, blah, blah, of those hockey bunnies that hung around the games. I grunted and shrugged. It was exhausting being a pig, but there was no way I was going to give her a way in. I couldn't do that. There was too much at stake. I had to protect *us*.

Passing wind would be too much, even I was above that, so I belched. A good squelchy one that drew some looks from the other tables. What was with these fucking tables, anyway? My knees were practically lifting it up off the floor. I flashed a glance at her, and she looked suitably unimpressed. This would be over soon.

Sarah

The smell of beer and chicken wings drifted across the table to my nostrils with a loud belch and I felt embarrassed. Yes,

I was embarrassed, not him. I wouldn't have been surprised if he kicked his shoes off and put his feet on the table.

What I was watching was an untrained, unkempt dog in human form. The only surprising thing was that he actually used his fingers to eat and didn't just put his face into that platter of chicken wings and go at it like a wild animal.

"Hey," I said jovially, smiling like I was actually enjoying myself, "You ever eaten at Jax's Chicken in mid-town? Finish a whole bucket in ten minutes and you get all your drinks for free. I think you'd be in with a shout! They also have my favorite chicken sandwich in town, the Chick'n'Go, and their Caramel Dreams milkshake is just, uhhh, to die for."

Hayden looked up at me blankly, like I'd asked him the square root of pie, sticky sauce smeared across his lips and drizzled on his beard, chicken between his teeth. It was official. My dream date was a nightmare.

I'd rather be home, watching television, drinking chilled wine, and eating flamin' hot Cheetos in my pajamas.

"Why did you even agree to this?" I finally asked, somberly and deflated.

"It's in my contract," he said dismissively as he threw another chicken wing on the pile of bones that was growing between us by the second.

"You know, I sold my car and pawned my grandma's ring for this," I said sadly.

For a moment, he stopped gnawing on wings and looked over at me sympathetically, his eyes softening from black holes into deep warm pearls, his jaw half-opening to say something. Then it slammed shut, the blank stare returned, and he chugged down his third beer in one enormous gulp. The rage swelled up in me as I looked at his face.

"You know, I really thought you were something Hayden

Raynor, but you're just another entitled selfish bum with no feelings and a crap beard!"

He looked surprised, which was the biggest reaction I'd had all night. Then he threw the last of the stripped chicken bones onto the plate, spread his huge arms out, like an eagle about to take off, and yawned.

"We done?" He said, after he finished showing me how bored he was.

"Sure," I hissed back.

"Cool. See ya then!" And he was already out of his chair and walking away, stopping to give his autograph with a wide grin to two excited young women on the way out.

I took out my phone and looked at it. There were five messages, all of them from Kensy.

> Hey, don't do anything I wouldn't do. If he wants a three-way, call me ;)
>
> Call me after your date! I want to know everything!
>
> Don't order the fish!
>
> Eye contact... Lots of eye contact!"
>
> I'm sooooo jealoussssssss!

"Excuse me, ma'am. The check."

I looked up as the waiter dropped the bill down on the table, before leaving me there alone. As I glanced around, a few of the other couples quickly looked away with amused smiles.

My humiliation was complete. I didn't have a car to go home in, or even a cab fare left after the $300 bill I now had to pay. All just to watch Hayden *fucking* Raynor eat ten pounds of chicken wings.

8

HEY CHAMP

Hayden

"Daddy!"

"Hey champ, what you still doing up?"

"Joyce said it was okay. I had a nightmare!"

"Oh no! You got spooked?"

"Yeah, but it's okay now. I'm glad you're home."

"I'm glad too buddy."

Joyce came into the hallway with a sweet smile on her lips, "So, how was your date?"

"It wasn't a *date,* Joyce," I rolled my eyes. "You know you're the only woman in my life."

"Oh, speaking of that, Cara called."

I sighed and rubbed a paw against my eye. *Christ, that hurts.*

"And what did she want?"

"Um, she was mad about some car payment she was expecting from you. Also, she can't take Maiden next weekend."

Joyce gave me a sad look. Honestly, that woman. Not

Joyce! She's been Maiden's nanny since the start, and she's some kind of gift from God. Cara is who I mean. And by *mean*, well, that's one of many words you could use to describe my soon-to-be ex-wife.

"Okay, thanks Joyce. I got it from here."

"I'm going to stay in the guest room tonight if that's okay? It's pretty late."

"Sure. Thanks again, I really appreciate it."

9

NEVER, EVER AGAIN

Sarah

"Get out!" I yelled, as my brain conjured up its familiar favorite image of Hayden Raynor, pulling back the shower curtain to give me a scrub down and a good morning seeing to.

How could he be such an oaf! How could I be so STUPID?

I went to grab my body scrub and winced painfully when I saw the naked finger where my grandma's ring used to be.

Never meet your heroes, they say. Well, I hadn't exactly met my hero, but I had met my crush, and it had been a titanic disaster. And now, I couldn't even enjoy my indulgent fantasies of him.

As dumb as it sounds, those fantasies were enough to keep me going. They helped me forget about the reality of my sad, lonely, and loveless life. Now, all of it was ruined. I fucking *hate* Hayden Raynor!

Just as I was stepping out of the shower, the doorbell

echoed through the hallway and I grabbed a towel before padding through the kitchen to answer it.

"Hi Kensy." Her face looked back at me, bright with excitement.

"Well!?" she said, unable to contain herself.

"It was... Oh, Kensy, it was awful!" I said, before my lip wobbled and the tears came.

"Oh God! Sarah, it's okay," her arms wrapping around me.

"No, no, it's not!" I wailed into her dress.

When I finally stopped sobbing so hard, Kensy took my hand and led me into my bedroom.

"Let's get you together, okay?"

I nodded, feeling like a child. As I got dressed and brushed the tears off my cheeks, Kensy asked delicately, "Did he... Do anything to you?"

I would've wondered the same, seeing the state I was in.

"God, no! Nothing happened. He was just the rudest, most awful person I've ever met. Then he left me at dinner with the bill and no way home."

"Oh God. That's terrible."

All I could do was nod as I went to re-apply the makeup that now looked like an artist's palette smeared across my face.

Kensy put her hands on my shoulders and looked at me intensely. "Okay, *fuck* Hayden 'dipshit' Raynor. You are an amazing woman, an incredible teacher, and you took a risk, and it didn't work out. I'm so proud of you. And you'll *never* have to see that man again."

10

EVER AGAIN

Hayden

"Is the new school going to be bigger than the old one?" Maiden asked from the backseat.

"Actually, it's gonna be smaller, champ. But you'll make lots of new friends. It's gonna be so much fun."

"Okay," Maiden said quietly, a stressed look spreading across his face. "Daddy? I feel weird in my tummy."

"Aw, you know what? That's how I feel before every hockey game."

"Really?"

"Yup! But then I just remember my name and that I'm strong and awesome and I don't need to be scared of anything. Now, what's your name?"

"Maiden."

"Maiden what?"

"Maiden Raynor!"

"Yeah! And who's strong and awesome?"

"Maiden Raynor!"

"That's right! We don't need to be scared, because we're 100% awesome!"

Maiden smiled and looked half-happily out of the window. I remembered how hard it was to move schools as a kid. The fear of fitting in, of getting teased for my size or my looks. I was a big kid even at Maiden's age, and if you stood out, you were a target. I guess that's why I got into so many fights. That, and the fact that my father prepared me for violence at a young age. I shuddered and quickly shook off the dark feelings that just the thought of that man gave me. Maiden might have had to put his fists up—the very reason why we had to change schools mid-term—but at least he didn't have to take a beating at home too.

The sign for Parkford Junior Primary School came up and we took the turn, "So, here's your new place, Raynor Junior. Looks nice!"

Maiden and I were looking out the window, seeing the school for the first time, when I had to slam my brakes on hard to avoid hitting two women who stepped out in front of the truck.

"Hey, watch it!" I yelled out of the window.

One of the faces staring back at me was familiar... *Susan? Saranda?* Damnit, what was her name? The one from last night.

After an uncomfortable moment of them gawping at me open-mouthed, they both finally stepped away from the front of my truck and I quickly drove on through the parking lot. In the rear window I saw them both turn, still wide-eyed and open-mouthed, their eyes following me.

"What the hell?" I muttered.

"What's that Daddy?" Maiden chirped.

"Nothing champ, let's get you to your new school."

Sarah

"Was that...?" I mumbled to Kensy.

She looked back at me with wild bulging eyes, "Uh-huh."

My eyes narrowed and the anger in my blood began to boil at the thought of that rude, arrogant, and self-entitled monster.

"What in the *hell* is he doing here?" I muttered.

"Perhaps you made more of an impression on him than you thought?" Said Kensy, hopefully.

The black look I gave her back told Kensy everything she needed to know. Furious at having to see his big, obnoxious, blockhead again, I watched the truck turn a corner in the parking lot, then made my way into the school, seething.

Inside the staff room, I got to the coffee pot just in time to watch Hicks pour the last drop into his cup.

"Oh, sorry Sarah," he smiled at me.

"Yeah, it's okay. It's the cheapest coffee in the world. I'm not even sure it's not painted rice, to be honest."

"Sarah, a word please?" Jill's voice was unmistakable. The sound of someone trying to sound more above their station than they really are.

She waited for me to come to her, even though she could just as easily come to me in the first place. It was a matter of principle. Being as she *was* the principal.

"We have a new one starting today. Had a bit of trouble at his last school, but his father made a rather helpful donation to our library fund, and I'm sure we can handle him."

"Uh-huh," I nodded back. Just what I needed today, an unruly new kid to disrupt the class. Jill looked at the sheet of paper in her hand.

"Erm, Maiden Raynor."

I stared at her.

"Oh, is there a problem?"

"No. It's just, I thought you said... Hayden Raynor?"

"Ah, no, it says here Maiden Raynor. He's outside with his father in the hallway if you could introduce yourself?"

I knew what was happening, but it was so unbelievable that I couldn't quite actually conceive it was true. I *had* to be mistaken. This couldn't be... I turned the corner and there he was, wearing that same stupid face that he had when we first met. Annoyingly gorgeous, and massive turd, Hayden Raynor. His ham hock of a hand resting on the shoulder of an awkward and shy-looking boy.

So, the brute had multiplied, just what we all needed.

"Hey. Um, didn't we?" Hayden started to say, uncomfortably.

Ignoring the half-grinning ogre that seemed to be blocking out every inch of sunlight, I kneeled down and smiled at the little boy who was trying to hide behind him, putting myself at his level.

"Well, hi there."

"Say *hi* Champ," the big ape said from above us, looking down at the nervous boy clinging onto his trouser leg. He managed a shy wave before burying his face back into his dad's pants.

"It's Maiden, right?"

A little nod.

"I'm Sarah, and I'm so excited to meet you! Do you like dinosaurs, Maiden?" I said, noticing the stegosaurus pattern on his shirt.

"He LOVES 'em! Don't you champ?"

I glared up at Hayden and he looked back at me, quickly understanding his interruptions were not welcome.

"Well, we've got LOTS of dinosaurs here. You want to come see them?"

Maiden looked hesitant, but the idea of dinosaurs was too big a pull and he let go of his dad's leg and turned to me, nodding.

"Oh, I can't wait to show you! My favorite one is Marvin. He's a stegosaurus. Let's go see, okay?" I stood and offered my hand and he took it.

I noticed Hayden's expression as we turned. A worried and concerned look. I'd seen a glimpse of it at our dinner. Now, it was painted across his big, stupid face as he watched his child walk away.

I wasn't sure it could get any worse. As it turned out, it only took half a day before there was trouble.

11

SCREAMING

Sarah

The screaming was the first thing I heard. When you teach kids, you get a good ear for the different types of screams. Like bird-songs to the trained ear, you can pick them out. This one was a serious cry, with pain involved.

Rushing outside, while the kids ran to press their faces against the window, I saw Hicks pulling Maiden up by his shirt, his face red and wild as he thrashed around trying to get free. Then I saw Kensy go to the floor where Matthew Lockley was bawling. His face a shocked mess of snot, tears, and blood.

Maiden was still flailing as he was dragged away by Hicks, while the other kids looked on as if they were watching a grown-up television show they didn't fully understand, but couldn't look away from.

As I got to the scene, Kensy was asking Matthew what happened. Between sobs, he was trying to tell her.

"He... He hit me... In my F... Fff.... Face," he wailed.

I crouched down next to Kensy, and we shared a concerned look.

"Why Matthew?" I asked him.

"I just said he... He... He... Couldn't read," then he looked at me in earnest, "Because he can't!"

"He can read just fine, Matthew. Why would you say that?" Kensy asked as she mopped up his snotty face with a tissue.

"He didn't know the... The... The number on the hopscotch... Then he HIT me!"

Back inside, Hicks had Maiden sitting on a chair in the hallway and was telling him, "You can't just hit people, Maiden. Why did you do it?"

Maiden just stared at the floor, his eyes thick with angry tears.

"We'll have to tell your dad, you know? What will he think?"

Maiden's head slumped further forward, and he put it in his big hands.

"Hey, Hicks. Let me talk to him."

Hicks looked up at me with a cross face, sighed, and then nodded. "Okay. I'll go and tell Jill what happened."

I kneeled down and Maiden looked back at me, his face distressed, scared, and confused.

"You know what you did wasn't okay, don't you, Maiden?"

He nodded and tried to swipe at the tears running down his face. *Trying to be strong,* I thought. That had his dad written all over it.

He didn't seem like a bad kid, though. Obviously, he didn't want this to be happening, so why was it?

"Hey, come with me. We can chat about it over dinosaurs, okay?"

It didn't cheer him up any, but he still nodded, just glad of something other than sitting in a hallway being told he was a bad kid. We sat on two tiny chairs in the playroom, him sniffling and me watching him.

"Maiden. Matthew said you didn't know the numbers on the floor. Is that true?"

He flashed an even brighter red than before and avoided looking at me.

"It's okay, you know. Just tell me. Or... How about you tell Marvin?"

I held up the plush toy stegosaurus and he looked at it. Once he realized that Marvin wouldn't judge him and didn't care about the stupid numbers either, he took it from me.

"Sometimes they get all jumbled and I don't like it when people say I'm stupid."

"The numbers?" I said.

He nodded. "And sometimes the words."

"Well, what about these?" And I pointed to the colored numbers on the playroom wall.

"They're okay."

"So, what was different with the numbers outside?"

"It's when it's all in a rush and I can't think proper."

"Like when you're playing a game?"

"Yeah. Or if I have to answer fast in front of the class. It's different then."

He looked like the saddest boy in all the world right then. I didn't even feel that sorry for Matthew Locklear, in all honesty. He was loud and annoying and a bit of a bully, just like his dad, but we couldn't be sending kids home to their parents their kids with black eyes and split lips.

"I see."

He started sobbing again, "W... Will my dad have to come and get me?"

"Oh. Probably. But hey, let's try and sort this out, okay? Let me talk to the principal and we'll see."

Kensy came in to join us while Marissa, the new teaching assistant, took Matthew off to the bathroom to get cleaned up.

"Hey, have you met Kensy yet? She'll look after you for a minute, while I go see what's happening, okay? You wait here with Kensy and Marvin."

Maiden nodded, and I gave Kensy a look that said *I feel bad for him, so go easy,* and she nodded her understanding back at me. Neither of us were moms, but we probably knew as much, if not more, about kids' behavior than the best of them.

Jill and Hicks were pulling sighing faces as I went into her office.

"Is he contained?" Jill asked.

"Contained? It wasn't a prison break, Jill. He's fine. Just in a bit of a mess."

"I've called his father already. He's on the way," she told me. "I should have known it was a bad idea."

"What are you going to do about it?" I asked back.

"We can't have our children threatened by violence, even if their father is a donor to the school. We have to set an example. He's been here, what? Four hours?"

"Jill. Look, I don't think he's a bad kid. Matthew was teasing him about not being able to read the numbers on the playground. I don't think anyone's ever understood or tried to help him. He's confused and embarrassed."

"Well, that's not how he should have reacted," she said bluntly, and now it was my turn to sigh.

She was right, of course, but how many times had this kid been moved on because no one had helped him learn how to control himself?

"Jill, don't get me wrong, what he did was really bad, but I think we could actually help this kid, not just throw him to the next school. Isn't that a better example to set? We're meant to be helping these kids learn, but also learn how to deal with life and human interactions."

"Sarah, I love the idea, but…"

"What about we give him a week? If I can get him and Matthew to make up and be friends, and he stays out of trouble, then we can move on."

"Sorry, but Matthew's parents will be all over me on this. They'll ask for him to be removed."

I thought of the Locklears for a moment and then realized we had a winning hand. It wasn't one I really wanted to consider, but at that moment, I was only thinking about the poor boy who needed some help from all these grown-ups who were ready to just brush him under the carpet.

"The Locklears will be okay with it," I told her.

Jill stared at me like I was mad. "Tom Locklear is not the kind of man to have a reasonable conversation, in case you don't remember his outbursts at the last teacher-parent evening?"

"I know, I know! But do you remember what he was wearing that evening, Jill?"

She thought for a moment before she recalled, "Oh, a football shirt, wasn't it?"

"No. Jill, it was a hockey shirt. An Ice-Hawks one at that. If Maiden's dad wants him to stay, then all he's gotta do is go apologize to Tom, maybe throw him some game tickets, and he'll lap it up."

Hicks had been quiet up until this point but spoke up. "Actually, that's not the worst idea I've ever heard."

Jill considered the scenario for a moment before deciding.

"If, and I mean, *if*, Tom accepts an apology, then he can stay. But the first sign of trouble after that, then he has no place at Parkford. Sarah, seeing as it's your idea, you talk to the father when he gets here."

An image of Hayden throwing another ravaged chicken bone on the table and then belching flashed across my mind.

"Oh! I really think it would come best from the principal, don't you?"

"I don't know any of this sports stuff. You seem to know about it. Just tell him what needs to happen."

12

SOLVING

Hayden

I couldn't believe it. How could Maiden, the sweetest, coolest kid in the world, have ended up in this situation? The obvious answer came to me, and I shuddered in sickening annoyance. His Dad beat people up all the time. *Was he just trying to be like me? His good old dad, who smashes people in the face all the time. It was true. It was me. I did this.*

I honked my horn and yelled some expletives at an SUV that came powering down the freeway in front of me. *Yeah, what a great role model you turned out to be Hayden. Another Raynor that talks with his fists.* At least I'd found somewhere I could do it where it was actually appreciated. But all I'd really done was repeat the mistakes of the past, and now Maiden was following that well-beaten path.

Could we handle another school? How many were even left that would take a kid whose biggest strength was a mean right hook? I took a sip from my travel mug and looked at the writing on it. *Best Dad In The World*. At that moment, I felt like the worst dad in history.

She was waiting for me outside the school and I felt a sinking feeling swimming in my guts. She probably couldn't wait to tell me that my kid was a monster like his dad and for us both to get the hell out of there. At least she'd have a story for her school teacher friends to tell over and over to each other.

Her arms were crossed and her expression serious as I got up to the school gates.

"Hi, where is he?"

She tried to hide her disgust of me, but made a bad job of it.

"He's inside and he's okay. But, look, can we talk?"

"If this is about the other night..."

"It's not," she said bluntly.

It was then that I remembered her name. *Sarah*. That's what she'd said when we'd met. I'd liked the way she'd said my name that night. It sounded nice.

We sat on the bench outside the front of the school and Sarah filled me in. How had I not noticed that all this time my own kid had, what? Learning difficulties? But, at the same time, I felt long-forgotten feelings of my own coming back, and then I knew why, and it made me even more mad at myself.

That feeling of confusion in school, when it felt like your brain was locked up and frozen and you couldn't match up the thoughts. They didn't have names or terms for it back then, unless you included *dumb* or *knucklehead*.

Sure, there had been frustration and embarrassments and fights and trouble, but that was all because of my old man, wasn't it? Or was there more going on back there that I had been hiding between the beatings? It was all just a haze of mixed-up feelings and painful memories that I couldn't fully unravel.

I guess I had hidden it well. Perhaps *too* well. I was a hockey head. That was all that mattered. So, it was no big deal, I just wasn't book-smart was all. When I started playing hockey, I didn't look back on any of it. I had my release. A world where you didn't have to do math tests or read in front of people. I was only graded on how well I played the game, nothing else. If someone had noticed, helped me... Well, maybe I'd have seen it in Maiden before it got to this.

"Hayden, I was wondering, where does Maiden's name come from? Is it Germanic?" She asked.

"Germanic? Um. No. It's from the rock band."

She paused. "You mean... *Iron Maiden*?"

"Yeah."

I noticed a small smile appear on her lips that she quickly disguised.

"Well, okay then. Let's go get Maiden," Sarah told me. Her features were so soft, I felt a pang in my chest when she looked at me. She made me feel different to anyone else I'd ever spent time with. Like she was really looking at you, really listening, not just thinking about what she wanted from you.

As we walked into the school, the other girl I'd nearly run over in the parking lot earlier that morning came over with Maiden.

"Hey there Champ," I said uneasily, my heart breaking as I looked at his sad face.

Maiden stared down at his shoes, expecting trouble.

"Don't worry, we're gonna sort this out. Me and your teacher think we can make it better for everyone, okay?"

Maiden nodded.

"First, we gotta go make some things right and take some responsibility. Okay?"

Sarah

Maiden looked up at me through his wet eyes.

"Are you not going to be my teacher anymore?" He asked, looking stressed and upset and still gripping tightly onto Marvin.

"Oh, I think me and your dad can figure something out, but we'll see, okay?"

It wasn't a "no" at least, and he nodded somberly.

"Hey, why don't you take Marvin with you? Look after him for me, then I'll have to see you again to get him back, won't I?"

Now he smiled.

So did Hayden. He looked annoyingly handsome when that pig-headed man smiled at his son. I'd met a lot of shitty parents and maybe he wasn't so bad. He obviously loved that kid like nothing else.

"Hey," I watched Hayden rub the back of his neck with a big paw as he spoke, comforting himself, "Just wanted to say, well, y'know, thanks. For Maiden. No one's really looked out for him before like this. Honestly, I don't know how we'd do it, finding another school. Not again."

He looked different now. The big, strong, belligerent hockey player was suddenly now a concerned dad. Worried and thoughtful and caring. He was still a giant jerk, but at least he showed he had *some* feelings.

"He's a good kid Hayden. We'll try and get him on the right track," I told him.

"You promise?"

I closed my eyes and nodded sincerely. When I opened my eyes again, he looked so sad and forlorn that my instincts were to go and hug him, to tell him it would all be okay. Instead, he just said in a shy kind of way, "Thanks Sarah," and walked away with his big slumped shoulders.

I smiled to myself. So, he *did* know my name.

I'd already half-turned when I heard his voice again from down the corridor, "Um, look..."

He was stood awkwardly leaning on one foot as I waited for him to say whatever it was on his mind.

"That night," he sighed, "I know it was awful. I guess I put it on a bit. These *women*..." He began to roll his eyes and wave his hand at how ridiculous *women* were. Then he caught my glare and quickly backed down.

"What I mean is... I can't have another puck bunny coming into our lives and messing us all up. It's not good for Maiden."

"Puck bunny?" I asked.

"Oh... Yeah. It's just what some of the guys call 'em. But, look, I didn't know you were, well, *normal*. So, yeah. I'm sorry. I guess."

"Okay, Hayden."

It didn't make it okay, not by a long shot. But the apology was appreciated. Maybe there was hope for the *Hellraiser* yet.

"Y'know, I don't date. It's me and Maiden and that's it. But, you seem so nice and I feel bad. I'd be happy to take you out one time to try and make up for it."

Wait. Did he just ask me out?

"Just to be clear, I don't date. Just friends, okay?"

Okay, no. He definitely did not.

I should've told him that he didn't deserve it and right where he could shove his offer, but I didn't. This other side of him was so vulnerable that it felt like talking to a completely different person.

"Well, I'm not paying for you this time, okay?"

He chuckled and relaxed a little when I didn't just tell him to go fuck himself.

"Yeah, okay. No bidding wars, just a drink. There's a place on Calverton where no one really bothers me. It's not quite as upmarket as the other night, but..."

"Do they do chicken wings?"

"Um, actually they do."

"Good," I said, smiling at him.

He smiled back, and I hated myself that my tummy fluttered with butterflies when he did. Stupid, handsome, pigheaded Hayden Raynor.

"So, tomorrow at like six? Place is called Freddy's."

"Alright then, I'll see you there. Have a good evening, Hayden Raynor."

"You too, Sarah."

For a moment, we stood there looking at each other. There was a discussion going on between us that neither of us could fully understand. It wasn't with words, it was something deeper. Some universal vibrations passing between us both, our most animal of instincts assessing each other as either a potential mate or a threat. The verdict was still unclear.

"Bye," Maiden said, breaking *whatever-the-hell-that-was* up.

"Bye," I said, blushing at the strange feelings I felt rushing in my blood.

13

THE APOLOGY

Hayden

"Jeez," I whistled as I drove up to the Locklear's house. *House* was too small a word. It was like driving up to the goddamn state capitol as we cruised up the driveway and past the perfectly manicured lawns.

"Let me do the talking, okay Champ?"

Maiden nodded his agreement from the backseat, looking uncomfortable at the boastful surroundings. We reached the entrance and, just as I slowed down, we were suddenly greeted by two wild, mean-looking rottweilers from hell, hurtling out of the house in full attack mode.

"Christ!" I yelled, veering manically away from the snapping, snarling jaws that flew at my window, taking my truck straight into the side of a parked red Porche. The awful sound of scraping metal made me wince as the hate-crazed beasts pounced and smeared the window with teeth and drool, showing me their meanest side.

"Jethro! Denver! Get here!" came the yell from a red-faced, plump, and enraged man who followed through the same door that the terror dogs had come from.

Jethro and Denver looked disappointed as they reluctantly stopped their assault on the unknown vehicle and trotted sheepishly back toward their owner.

"My fucking car!" The angry potato screamed, holding his hands to his head and pulling at where his hair would've been, if he had any.

Fuck. This had not started well.

Climbing out of the truck, I looked down at the red-faced figure in front of me and his expression softened in surprise.

"Hayden Raynor?" He asked.

I nervously rubbed the back of my neck. "Er, sure is. Mr. Locklear?"

"That's right," he said, gawping at me like I'd just levitated in front of him.

"Damn, I'm real sorry about that," I told him, looking uncomfortably at the tangled mess of cars. "Your dogs came out at me like a wild one. I'll, er, get that fixed."

"Sure, sure. Hey, come on in!" He'd remarkably cheered up now and didn't seem that concerned by the fact my truck was chomping into his Porsche, exactly like his dogs had wanted to do with my leg.

Maiden and I followed the blob into the inner-sanctum of his palace, walking through a reception room of garish old paintings, with wide, opulent staircases running up either side of the hallway. Then, we were led out onto a sun-soaked terrace, where we found a group of middle-aged people lounging lazily, while screeching kids ran around an Olympic-sized pool.

"Hey! Look who's here! Hayden fucking Raynor!" That's how Locklear introduced me to his gin-soaked audience.

The oldest of them, perhaps Locklear's mother at a guess, didn't even turn her head, but just sighed. She looked like old money and unimpressed by everything. Meanwhile, a guy in a sports cap (Wildcats, I mean *really?*) got up awkwardly, nearly fell back down, reclaimed his balance, and then came over, beaming.

"Jesus, you're massive!"

I nodded back at him. "Er, thanks?"

"Hey, you know Randall Jackson, right?"

The Randall Jackson who plays on my team? I mean, I might.

"Yeah, sure I know Randall."

"I heard... *It's* massive."

I frowned back at his shining eyes. Was he really asking me, a man he'd just met for the first time, the size of Randall's cock? The fact he was still staring eagerly and wobbling in front of me as he waited for my answer, told me he actually was.

"Oh." I took my cap off and scratched at my head. *Gotta play it nice here Hayden, for Maiden, remember? And then there's that Porsche outside. Better give them a bit of a show.* "Well... You know Jessa Huckley?"

Everyone knew Jessa. The former Playbunny turned good girl, then back to getting her assets out again. She and Randall had been a thing. It was short-lived, but the gossip columns had lapped it up.

"Yeah, I do!" He sounded pleased with himself.

"Well, let's just say they broke up because he wasn't that *in*to her." I held up my hand and wiggled my pinky finger to illustrate what I meant. It was nice to get one over on Randy, even if he wouldn't ever find out about it.

Sports cap guy's eyes bulged and then he burst into a wild laughter that made me recoil, as if he'd just opened his mouth and moths had flown out of it.

Locklear whacked me heartily on the back and started laughing too.

"DAD!"

We all turned toward the interruption, which came from a small blonde kid sporting a hell of a black eye on his face and a white plaster across his nose. Maiden squeezed my hand harder.

"Can we go on the golf cart?"

"No, Matthew! Not after the last time."

Matthew looked like he was about to throw a tantrum, then he turned to peer up at me.

"You're that hockey player."

"Sure am!" I told him as cheerfully as I could muster. Did these rich folk just go around stating obvious facts all the time? Was that a thing? *Oh hey, you're wearing a shirt. Oh look, it's a tree. This is my enormous swimming pool.*

After a pause, an excited expression came across his face. "Can you throw me in the pool?"

I looked over at his dad to see what his thoughts were on that, and he just shrugged. So I leaned over, picked up the blonde kid, held him up over my head like I was a pro-wrestler, and chucked him unceremoniously into the pool. The other kids stood for a moment open-mouthed, then they started running toward me, all yelling at the same time, "Me next! No, me! Do me!"

I managed an hour of throwing kids in the pool, making idle chat with Tom Locklear and the Wildcats fan, whose name I never got, and getting withering looks from Tom's mother before we made our escape. I would've made up an excuse to get us out of there once everything had been smoothed over, but I actually had one already. One I didn't really want to think about. Cara.

14

CLARA'S SHEEP

Hayden

This was becoming a real day of it. After dealing with Maiden's fallout and becoming Locklear's show pony, I then had to drop Maiden at soccer practice (seriously, what was up with that?), get to my state-enforced therapy session that afternoon, and then there were drinks lined up after that to win over the teacher.

On top of it all, Cara, my living nightmare, was about to bring her special brand of hell back into our lives, despite everything I had tried to do to avoid it. It was always bad news. Every time a woman came into our life.

"Daddy, are we stopping at Ice-Cream Dreams?" Maiden called out from the backseat.

"Sorry champ. We're late to pick up your mom."

"Okay." I glanced at Maiden's sad face in the rearview mirror and my heart broke for him. *That damn woman.* Three days and then it would be just him, me, and Joyce again.

"Why's mom staying with us?" Maiden asked.

I sighed heavily. Me and Cara had made a deal. I hadn't wanted to, but that hell-spawn in heels knew *exactly* how to manipulate me, and every time I found myself dancing around like a bear in a tutu to her tune.

"I just need to stay at the house, two days, three tops," she'd told me. Cara never asked for anything. She just told you what you would do for her. How much money you'd send, what bill to pay, what party she needed a pass for, whatever she wanted.

"No way. There is absolutely no chance in hell, Cara!" I'd told her as defiantly as I could.

The woman had no scruples, though.

"Look Hay-Ray," I *hated* when she called me that, and she knew it too, "I let you have your quiet, boring life with Maiden and your lame stick buddies, but that can change very quickly, you hear me? You still in therapy for your anger, by the way?"

My cheeks had burned. I knew exactly what she meant by that therapy jibe. She could take Maiden any time she wanted. I had no bargaining power here.

"Two days, tops," I'd told her coldly, at least trying to salvage something and not just be kicked around by her.

"Three days. Unless you want me to stay longer? I could do a couple of weeks instead. I mean, it is *my* home and *my* kid too, Hay-Ray."

And that was that. I knew when I was beaten. If I pushed my luck, she would just make it worse for me.

"And pick me up from the airport. I land at two."

So, there we were. Going to help the one person in the goddamn world that I would rather push off a bridge. I groaned as we hit the airport traffic that slowed us to a crawl.

"It's just a few days, Champ. Don't you wanna see your mom?"

Maiden's silence answered the question.

"Makes two of us," I muttered under my breath.

Cara was late. Nothing new there. You always had to wait around for her. Finally, she emerged, swaggering through the departure gate like a movie star in white gloves and dark shades, with two athletic-looking college kids pushing carts of her designer luggage that she'd roped in from somewhere.

"Darlings!" she exclaimed in a faux-British accent as she air-kissed me extravagantly.

"Yeah. We're late, so let's get going Cara," I huffed back at her.

"Aw, so pent up. You really need to relax a little Hay-Ray."

If I'd wanted to do weights, Cara's bags were as good as any.

"Do you need all this?" I asked as I loaded the cases into the trunk. "I thought it was a flying visit."

"Better to be prepared, isn't it?" Cara said, putting her hands on Maiden's shoulder. I smirked a little, seeing him shrink away from her clutches.

"Do we need to tip them?" I nodded toward her cart pushers.

"Oh, no. These gentlemen were just kind enough to help a frail young woman out. Isn't that right, boys?"

The two guys shyly beamed back at her while flashing nervous glances at me, before Cara dismissed them with a wave of her white leather-gloved hand.

"Sure," I sighed, "Let's get going."

"Oh, let's stop at Handerson's. I need something to match the perfume I got at the airport."

"How do you match bags with perfume, exactly?" I snorted back at her.

"You wouldn't understand," she said with an air of superiority. "It's a taste thing."

"Oh, how I've missed you Cara, but we can't stop. Maiden's got practice, then I've got... A thing."

Cara laughed, and I pursed my lips. Someone my size isn't used to being made to feel three-feet tall and stepped on. I never liked how she could do that to me.

"I hope you remembered to get my favorite ranch water in Hay-Ray."

"I did not. Get your own medication, Cara."

She sighed in annoyance, and I felt a small prickle of satisfaction.

"Guess we're stopping then."

"No! We're not stopping. I already told you."

"Hayden Raynor, more fun than Disneyland," she sneered back.

"Cut the..." I looked in my rearview at Maiden in the back, "...Sheep Cara, we don't need it."

"Like I need your *sheep* either, Hayden. You can't give me three frogging days to at least pretend to play nice?"

"Don't frogging push me, Cara. I've got enough sheep to deal with already, without your special brand of it."

"Way to make a girl feel special, you frogging animal."

Thankfully, she went quiet after that.

Just a few days, that's all...

15

ANGER MIS-MANAGEMENT

Hayden

So Dana, my therapist, she's cute enough, but cold as ice. Like she can't react to anything I say with any judgment. But I *know* she's judging me. The first thing I learned was that jokes don't go down well with that one. She just stares at me until I stop grinning and waiting for a response, and then says something like, "Let's get serious."

To be clear, I hate these sessions, but I don't really have a choice. My court-appointed therapy started after *that* incident last year. Cue a massive eye-roll. I mean, it was a fight at a hockey game, as in *my actual job!* The whole thing was ridiculous.

Okay. So, sure, I wasn't actually playing because of a hamstring strain, but I'm still gonna stick up for my teammates. Throw in the fact that he called me "Bellraiser" in the tunnel, and that explains why he got his head punched in. Long story short, but I got called out for assault, and now every week in the off-season I had to sit in the smallest, most goddamn uncomfortable, chair you've ever seen in your life and talk about feelings and stuff for an hour.

My only saving grace had been that the judge was a hockey fan and agreed it could only happen in the off-season, seeing as we were out on the road for half the rest of the year. Really messed up my summer plans, though.

"Hayden," Dana said, adjusting her dress. I'd seen this before. She probably fancied some of the bad boy in the seat across from her. "Do you think you're protecting Maiden from these women? Or are you really protecting yourself?"

I scoffed at the nerve of it.

"From what? Sniffing out every chance to fill their bank balance? Or making me feel like hell when all I want is to give my kid a life that isn't full of sheep... I mean, *shit*!"

"From getting hurt, Hayden. Your father was violent, your mother left you, Cara left you. You're hiding from love because you think it can only hurt you if you let it in."

My face turned crimson. I was not used to being talked to like this, and it was absolutely not what I wanted to hear. Who was *she* to be saying these things about *my* life? How could she ever possibly understand what it's like to be *me*?

"Even your work persona, the *Hellraiser*. It's a defense mechanism to push people away so you don't get hurt. You're pretending to be something big and scary, but even monsters need love, Hayden. It's what makes them become something more."

"Look, I *need* to be strong for Maiden!"

"I think you need to show him what *real* strength is Hayden. To be able to let people in to see your vulnerable side and take those risks, despite the fear."

I was furious now with this ridiculous second-hand parenting. *Taking risks? Having fear!?*

"You don't know *anything* about us!"

"Okay. Perhaps we can talk about something else."

"Yeah, I think we're done talking, *doctor*!"

I was spitting blood. Hopefully, she took my derogatory way of saying *doctor* as it was meant. She wasn't a real doctor, not one that mattered, one that actually saved people's lives. She'd also gone well over the line. Just another rich Daddy's daughter who had it easy her whole life. She didn't know what it was really like to grow up in that house, to be scared of going home after school, to try and sit still in class with bruises all over your ass because Daddy had one too many drinks, and you had to put yourself in the way, because it was either you or mom. I was still seething with anger and shame when I pulled open the door and stormed out of her office.

"Fuck!" I yelled as I hammered a fist down on the bonnet of a white Ford pickup outside the reception. The car alarm jumped into life and I yelled "Fuck!" again as I felt the pain reverberate in my fist.

I was so blinded with rage, all I saw was a blur of some small annoying man running outside in a bad suit and thick black glasses, talking to me like I was an idiot.

"Hey! That's my car!"

"So what! Fuck off!"

I started to walk away. I just wanted to go to a dark bar and sip on cold beers until the throbbing in my fist didn't hurt so bad.

"Hey! I'll call the cops, you animal!" He yelled after me.

I felt the red mist descend. Like it was game night and the mouthy forward who'd been winding me up all game had finally overstepped the mark. It was what I was trained for, it's what I did.

I turned, growling, and walked toward him. Things might have gone differently had he turned and run away, but the idiot just stood there as I got closer. My fist didn't hurt anymore as I put it square into his face. Nothing hurt anymore. I was the *Hellraiser*.

16

THE NON-DATE

Sarah

I arrived at Freddy's a couple of minutes late, in an effort to seem as casual as possible. Looking around, I was disappointed to find he hadn't turned up yet, so he couldn't see how relaxed I was about this. I wasn't. *Relaxed*, that is. My throat was dry, my heart was pumping way harder than it needed to be, and I really needed a drink. Waiting was *not* what I needed right now.

Ordering a Tom Collins, I settled down at a table and enjoyed the sensation of the cool drink soothing both my throat and my nerves as I sat, watching the door and waiting.

After everything, I was going to have my actual date with Hayden. Okay, *not* a date. He'd made that clear. I was also still reeling from the other night with that man, but if I'd have passed this up, I wouldn't have been able to stop thinking about it, and I was getting tired of regrets.

Fifteen minutes went by of me jumping nervously every time that damn door swung open. Flashing the same welcoming expression across my face at each new arrival, followed by a return to the frown that came with my increasing annoyance.

I checked my phone again, and there was nothing. I couldn't text him. That would give him the upper hand, and I wasn't prepared to do that at all.

By my third drink, I was starting to feel a little woozy, and I barely raised my head each time the door swung open. Sitting there on my own, I felt more and more embarrassed as time passed into the second hour of waiting. *Maybe he actually said seven, not six? Maybe he's in the worst traffic ever? Or an accident? I couldn't be mad if that was the case.*

As I sat there, the drinks working their way through my bloodstream, my hair beginning to lose its luster along with my spirit, I started to think about Jake.

I'll keep you safe forever...

"Pah!" I accidentally shouted out, quickly covering my mouth at the mistake, but no one seemed to notice.

Lucy... Garrett? Grantham? No, *Grayson*. That was her name. With her blonde hair, her sweet big-eyed face, her young, innocent smile, and her not-so-innocent skirts. *I hated her. She did this to me.*

Jake had been my mentor, a dashing, dark-haired older man who could make you blush just by looking right at you. When he had looked right at me, it wasn't like the rest of them, though. There was fire and heat in those looks, and I was not old or wise enough to know better. I'd fallen, and I'd fallen hard.

It had been my dream job. I was just an intern that first year, but I worked hard, people liked me, and it was nailed on that I would stay as a permanent member. Enviro-Tech was about as unglamorous a company name as you could imagine, but the work was anything but that. It felt like we could change everything, that we would provide cheap renewable electricity to communities that were war-ravaged, famine-ravaged, abandoned by their corrupt governments, and needing people like us to intervene.

The way Jake spoke about it made him seem like a messiah, leading us all to a better world. And we followed him with wonder.

I was helplessly in love with him. The first time he had put his hand on my shoulder as he leaned over to look at my work, there was more heat between us than anything I could have ever imagined. I'd go home and savor that touch, that face, and his divine scent when he came close to me.

It didn't take long before the spark became a fire, and it raged unstoppably.

We'd made love every chance we could get. Tearing at each other's clothes with annoyance at them keeping us from the prizes underneath. Desperate to touch, taste, and have every single inch of each other. It was never enough, we were always ravenous for more. Our hands would brush against each other at work, our eyes telling each other our wildest fantasies... *I have to have you... I need you... I need you NOW...*

I still had girlish traits. Being in that position of not being a girl anymore, but not quite experienced enough to fully be a woman, either. So, the journal I had kept changed, and instead became a hand-written shrine to him, full of gushing notes.

When I'm with Jake, it makes me feel like we're the only ones in the world... His cock is so perfect. It's like it was made just for me, and I was made just for him... When he sleeps I watch him and I know I've found everything, and I know he feels the same... I love it when I'm on top of him and he runs his hands through my hair, his eyes looking deep into mine, my hand pushing down on his beautiful chest as we gasp at each other. This is it. Real love...

I couldn't have seen it coming. I was too blinded with love. Intoxicated by every single thing he did and said. For me, it was all falling into place. I would get my dream job, my dream man, and my life was soaring in a way I couldn't have imagined.

There were signs, but I either didn't see them, or chose to ignore them. He would flirt a little with the other girls and they would stare at him gooey-eyed and laugh too hard at his jokes. But that was just him. It was his nature. None of those girls would be in his bed later, only me. Or so I thought.

Maybe I created my own downfall? Taken my eye off the prize a bit, was less hard-working, had less of a keen eye, because both of my eyes were distracted continually by him. I made mistakes at work that I wouldn't have before, but they were just minor things, and Jake would smooth them over. I was more curt to other staff members and the interns, because I was flying high and I didn't have the same time for them anymore. Only him.

It had been the fall of that year when the next intake of interns were to be announced and we would move on to our next roles, either in or out of the company. I wasn't worried. I felt secure already and ready for my new life to open its next wondrous chapter.

Gary Bradbury was the Chief Medical Director, and I went to see him in the afternoon to see what I would be working on next. I was still in disbelief as I left his office. *This must be a mistake?*

It's hard to remember his exact words as I stood there grinning at him, but they were something along the lines of... "Thanks for being a part of our mission here. I hope you've enjoyed the experience. Your internship ends next month and we would like to give you this letter of reference to help you toward finding your next position."

He held out the piece of paper to me and, still grinning but with a little less sparkle, I reached out to take it, wondering when he was going to tell me which role I would be given. He just stared at me, waiting for me to speak or leave, but it became clear that there was nothing else he had to say to me.

"But... I thought..." was all I could stammer.

He lifted his eyebrows, "Yes. Well, who knows what the future holds?"

My cute optimism was shelved as a dark anger rippled through me. Thankfully, I was still in enough of a daze that I turned and left his office without unleashing myself on him.

But... I thought...

My first instinct was to go and find Jake. He would get this all cleared up, maybe even go bursting into Gary Bradbury's office and demand he hire me without question or he, himself, would resign immediately. My heart fluttered at the idea of him protecting me, standing up for me.

The lab was quiet that day. The interns were only there to see Gary and then had the rest of the day to themselves. As I approached the swinging doors that reminded me of those in a kitchen restaurant, I saw his face through the crack and my heart jumped. Not just my heart. Maybe we could fit in a moment of wild passion before he came to my rescue. Then, there was someone else in my frame of vision, and they were looking at each other kind of funny.

Lucy Grayson.

Suddenly, everything spun when I saw her stand up on her toes and her hands slide onto his shoulders. My stomach felt like it was being ripped apart at the exact same moment as I watched her lips meet his. It was like poison had flooded my bloodstream, every inch of my body curling up in aching disbelief. The death of love and the birth of love, both occurring in two different people in the same place at the same time.

I heard their vague murmurings through the crack in the door.

...I can't wait for next year as your highly capable assistant Doctor...

...Are you sure you're comfortable working under me...

...More than comfortable, although sometimes I like to be on top...

I didn't go back for my last month. I just went home to my tiny room and cried and cried and cried. Three weeks later, broke and heartbroken, and having never felt more lost, I rode the Greyhound back to my hometown. Now, I'm sitting in a bar, having been stood up, feeling humiliated and completely alone all over again.

I picked up the phone and called Hayden's number. It rang out without an answer. A small self-pitying tear found its way down my cheek, before falling into my empty glass and onto the melting ice.

Fuck this. Fucking Hayden Raynor.

I picked up my jacket and ordered a cab.

17

CUSTODY

Hayden

By the time the squad car had pulled up, I'd regained most of my senses. It didn't stop the cops from pointing their guns and yelling at me to get down like I was top of "America's most wanted" list, though. To be fair, I'm a big guy and there was another guy screaming on the floor, covered in blood, next to me. I'd probably expect the worst too.

And yeah, if you're wondering, I *did* feel bad. That guy continued to cuss at me through the blood streaming from his nose, but he still didn't deserve this. Like I told Dana once, sometimes I felt like one of those Army vets, who have to contain everything they were trained for every day of their civilian lives, but there's always something there in the background waiting to snap. Except that the closest I'd been to Vietnam was a week's luxury vacation in Thailand. The therapy was supposed to help, but it had made things worse.

I heard Dana's cold, flat voice in my head, knowing what she'd say to that... *It's not the therapy that made it worse Hayden, it's you... Most people don't walk out of here and just start smashing cars and strangers... You threw a tantrum because you're scared of facing the truth...*

"Hey, easy!" I said as the aggressive little trooper roughly snapped his cuffs on me, while the other stood back, nervously pointing his firearm at me.

By now, there was a small crowd watching on. I guess Dana would've come out to see what was going on and I felt her judgment without even needing to see her disapproving face. *Please don't let this make the news,* I thought as they bundled me into the back of the squad car.

I had one call at the station. Who made up that damn rule, anyway? What if they didn't pick up? Or you dialed the wrong number? Or you had an especially large family?

It was an obvious choice, though. I had to get Maiden picked up from soccer practice and somehow let Sarah know I wouldn't be making it to Freddy's. So, instead of calling Sarah from a police station–*yeah Hayden, a great way to show your kid's teacher what a responsible role model of a parent you are*–I decided I'd call Joyce.

Joyce would pick up Maiden from practice, and I'd also tell her to call Sarah for me and say... Well... I didn't know yet, but Joyce was resourceful. She'd come up with *something*, an emergency team meeting, a plumbing issue, saving a kitten from a house fire, a mystery illness that had doctors baffled...

I called on the house phone. Joyce wasn't the kind to carry around her mobile 24/7, I liked that about her.

"Yeah, hullo?"

Shit. Cara. In all the fuss, I'd forgotten she was there.

"Uh, Cara, can you get Joyce for me?"

"Who is this, please?"

"You know who it is. Just get Joyce, please."

"Oh my, is this *The Hellraiser*?" she teased, cackling at her own amusement.

"Cara! Christ, just do it!"

"I mean I could. What you gonna do for me?"

"Nothing! This is important Cara, seriously!"

"Ooh, so it's *really* worth something. You know you caught me in the middle of looking through the latest Cartier line."

"Cara, I need Maiden picking up from practice, okay!? You know, your kid!"

"Alright, keep your pants on Hay-Ray. I'll pick him up. Then I'll let you know later what you can buy me in return."

With that, the line went dead before I could say anything else.

I slammed the phone down, ready to scream. Then I remembered Sarah. *Shit!*

"Oh, hey, I got cut off. I need to try again?" I said to the officer.

"No chance buddy. Let's go, there's a line."

I looked behind me to see one guy, swaying and babbling something about electric trains.

"What line? Him?" I pointed a thumb at the gremlin next to us.

"Don't get mouthy now. I don't make the rules."

Of course you don't... This day was getting worse by the second...

18

JIMMY, THE REPAIRMAN

Hayden

"Raynor!" My ears perked up from the cell. It was more spacious than the sin bin, didn't smell any better though, "You're out on bail."

Jimmy was waiting in the entrance for me and we gave each other a big smile. I don't know what I did to deserve that guy. We'd been friends since high school, abysmal hockey player, but a great teammate, and about the only person I really trust in this world. He's also my agent. I'd insisted he represented me since the start, despite his lack of experience. He was the only person I knew with a business degree that I knew would always have my back.

"You're coming with me," I'd told him when I really started getting noticed in hockey circles, and he'd thrown himself into it. Now he was one of the best in the business.

"Thank God you're here Jimmy. Cara call you?"

"Nope, caught you on the news, Hay. Figured you might need me, so I made a few calls and here we are."

Jimmy held up his phone to show me the clip doing the

rounds. There was me being held down and handcuffed, while a bloody-nosed man screamed blue murder in the background. Underneath was a revolving newsreel that read "Hellraising In Merryville."

Ugh. This was not a good look.

"We'll get the PR team on it, but for now, let's get you home."

"Maybe a cold one on the way? It's been a day."

"Tommys?"

"Gotta be."

If Jimmy was a good agent, he was a better friend. I was his enforcer of a different kind at high school. Some of the other kids had taken exception to him, seeing as his family was from the nicer end of town. I put a few of them straight and we were inseparable after that.

As we rode in his car across the city, I hit dial on Sarah's phone and waited until it rang out. What a jerk I was. She was well within her rights to hate me.

We rolled into Tommys and slid ourselves into a booth.

"Hay, should I be worried?"

"Nah, Jimmy, just got some things going on. Cara's back in town, Maiden's had some problems at school."

I checked my phone again and Jimmy gave me a look that said, *c'mon, we're friends, what are you not telling me?*

"What I mean Hay is I *am* worried. Who you waiting on a call from, anyway?"

I sighed heavily.

"Wait. Hayden. I know that look. It's the look of someone irrational, whose feelings are all mixed up good and proper. You met someone?"

"Nope. I just let someone down that I really didn't want to."

Jimmy shot me a grin that I rolled my eyes at.

"It's not that, Jimmy. It's just Maiden's teacher. She helped him out, and I was kind of... I was a massive jerk, is all."

"Uh-huh."

"Why are you looking at me like that?" I scowled back at Jimmy's odd smile. Jimmy knew me too well sometimes and, hell, I didn't know what I felt. Just that this isn't how I'd wanted things to go.

"So, you gonna do something about that?" Jimmy said.

I thought for a moment... "Actually, yeah. Jimmy, you want to run an errand with me?"

"Sure Hay, where we going?"

19

BUTTERMILK CHICKEN

Sarah

It felt good to take my make-up off, get out of my bra, and slump back in my sweats with a bottle of wine, a tub of Ooey-Gooey-Choco-Lava ice cream, and a classic movie.

As I settled in and turned on the TV, the news flashed on the screen and there he was. Not exactly in all his glory, but instead being dragged into a cop car.

Hayden Raynor. *So that's where you went tonight.*

"...Hayden 'the Hellraiser' Raynor was taken into custody for an alleged violent assault in Merryville this afternoon. Details are still coming in but the captain of the Ice-Hawks was caught on film by bystanders, just two days before the Mayor's Ball here in Merryville, where he was widely tipped to receive his MVP award from the Mayor himself..."

That was enough of Hayden for me tonight. Or for forever. I flicked over to the movie and settled in for a nice ten minutes, before a pounding on my door made me jump like hell. I wasn't in the mood for annoyed neighbors, unexpected guests, or mob hitmen right now. Who in the hell would it be at this time, anyway? The door strained under another round of thumping.

Throwing open the door, ready to yell at whoever was treating it as a punchbag at this time of night, there he was, filling up my entire doorframe. The dream. The nightmare. Hayden Raynor. I went to throw the door closed again, and one of his large paws reached out and stopped it.

"Hey! Wait, Sarah, please."

As I scowled at him for the intrusion, the way he'd made me feel *again*, the audacity of showing up here, I looked down at his hands and frowned, "Is that?"

"Um... Jax's milk butter chicken sandwich, curly kale fries, and a caramel dreams shake. Also threw in a mega-chicken-bucket just in case," he looked up at me earnestly, "I got it right, didn't I?"

Huh, so he actually did listen that night.

It would take a lot more than Jax's chicken to win me over, but there was this look in his eyes, like he was desperate to make it right, to change my thoughts on him. I felt my heart beat harder in my chest and was annoyed at it. I didn't want to feel anything for him.

"So, look..."

"Yeah, you got yourself arrested. After I was waiting for... Well, I waited long enough for you! Then I found out on the *fucking* news, Hayden."

As I wavered, he looked past me and saw the frozen image of Kevin Costner and Whitney Houston on the screen.

"The Bodyguard!"

"Oh!" I blushed, feeling judged.

"I love that movie!"

I couldn't tell if he was teasing me, until I saw his bright, excited eyes. *Oh my God.* He *actually* loves that movie...

I sighed. There was something about him that stopped me wanting to tell him off. I was too tired to be mad. I'd already been mad at him for hours before he'd unexpectedly turned up at my door, and it was exhausting.

"Well, gee! I guess come in then," I told him with a heavy dose of sarcasm and extended my arm to the apartment.

Hayden

Watching Kevin Costner trying to handle Whitney's shit, while chowing down on Jax's chicken (she was right, it was good!) and sipping chilled rosé, was about as good as an evening as I could have imagined. Why didn't everyone want to do this? All I got asked to do was to take people to some pretentious new club, a boring restaurant opening, or anywhere that celebrities might hang out. No one ever wanted to do *this*.

I looked over to check Sarah's expression, hoping she still wasn't quite so mad at me, but she was transfixed by the movie, her fingers moving food from the bucket to her mouth as if they were operating on another level.

She actually looked great without make-up. Those soft wrinkles around her eyes when she smiled were adorable. I leaned over to top up our wine glasses and sat back comfortably.

And you're ready to die for me?
It's the job.
And you'd do it. Why?
I can't sing.

Her lips curled in delight at those lines. Sarah noticed me looking and turned to me. I gave her a timid smile, hoping that she was at least enjoying this, despite everything. Hell, if I didn't feel so bad about letting her down, I was enjoying it, too. The rosé was slipping down nicely, making me feel warm and fuzzy. Those dimples in her cheeks when she moved her lips were really something. We both turned back to the movie.

What are you afraid of?
I'm afraid of not being there.

Sarah's hand went for the bucket, with mine already deep in there and, as we brushed each other's skin, something electric sparkled inside. The sensation sent a flickering rush of wild emotions that my brain had not anticipated, and neither of us moved our hands away. For a fleeting moment, they found each other and delighted in the touch before we pulled them away. It was odd afterward. Like my hand missed hers, and I wanted it to come back.

This time, I caught Sarah looking at me with an amused look on her face.

"What?" I asked.

"Hayden Raynor, drinking rosé and watching The Bodyguard. It's a surprise."

"Uh-huh," I said, fixing my eyes on the screen and feeling embarrassed, "Just don't tell anyone, okay?"

She laughed. "I'm not sure anyone would believe me."

Damn. Who laughs like that? There was no malice or upmanship. No game. It was just sweet and uplifting.

"So, what the hell happened tonight, Hayden?"

I sighed. For a blissful moment, I'd forgotten about the police, about Cara, Dana, and Locklear.

"It's just been a day. Look, Sarah, I'm really sorry you got caught up in it all. There's a lot going on."

She eyed me suspiciously, waiting to see if I'd continue. Something about her, or maybe it was the gas station rosé, made me want to tell her everything. I'll be the first to admit I'm guarded, but in my position, I have to be. Loose lips tend to come back to haunt me. That much I'd learned from Cara. Sarah was different, though. I didn't just know it, I could feel it.

"So, Maiden's mom turned up this afternoon. She always puts me on edge. Then I have to see this therapist, and between them both pushing my buttons, I just... Well, you saw, huh?"

"Yeah, it wasn't the best look, to be honest. And you stood me up! So, y'know, it's hard to be sympathetic."

I nodded ruefully. She was right. Thing is, I was the one who was used to being let down, but now it was me doing it to this lovely woman who didn't deserve any of it. I wanted to look at her again. *Why did I want to look at her again so badly?*

After a moment of silence, she changed the topic.

"So, you always wanted to be a hockey player?"

I was relieved to move on from my failings as an absolute ass-biscuit, "Sure. I mean, look at me, I was built for it."

I held up my forearm and flexed it for playful effect. But she didn't smile. Instead, her eyes just seemed to shine as she watched my bicep swell, before she snatched her look away.

Both our cheeks reddened, as if our inner thoughts might have been exposed, and we turned back to the movie. She didn't look at me as she asked the next question.

"Do you have a... Girlfriend, or a lover, or someone Hayden?"

"That never really works out for me."

"What does *that* mean?"

"Women come into our lives and make everything worse."

"Maybe it's just your choice in women, Hayden?"

Fuck. I loved it when she looked at me. Those crinkles at

the edge of her beautiful eyes made the world suddenly feel soft and light and perfect.

"Could be," I smiled back.

"What about Joyce, though? How does she fit into all this?"

I'd never told anyone too much about Joyce. It didn't feel right to share her story. It was *her* story, after all. It certainly wasn't something I was going to tell any of the guys or Cara about.

"Joyce is a saint, really. She was in a tough spot when we met. Hell, we both were. I mean, you should try dating Cara. She's not about to win any 'Mom Of The Year' awards."

"Yeah, I think I'll pass, but thanks for the heads up."

"Well, anyway, we helped each other out and she keeps me and Maiden on track. I guess she's the closest thing to a mom he has."

"And the closest thing you have to a wife?"

I hadn't really thought of it that way, but she was right. Joyce was our surrogate mother and wife, without being either.

"We're not together. Y'know, like *that*."

I felt like I had to make it clear and she nodded her understanding. God, it felt good to talk about stuff with her. Not like with Dana, certainly not with my teammates, or even worse, Cara. Jimmy was great, but we're guys. There's a line there that you only step over when you're about to break. And even then, you hate yourself a little bit afterward for being soft and vulnerable.

"How about you anyway?" I asked.

"Hah!" she threw back.

"Okay... So, is that a no, then?"

A sad expression came across her face and I just wanted

to put my hand on her chin, lift her head, turn it toward me, and look into those eyes to see everything behind them.

"Maybe I've just been waiting for you, Hayden."

She said it as a joke, but it came across differently. Something in her tone revealed more depth and meaning to it. We looked at each other, our eyes translating messages to our brains, a spark between us seeming to lock us together.

"Oh, wait! Here we go!" She exclaimed, spilling some of her wine in excitement.

I took a breath. There was no avoiding it. It was going to happen. We both took a last exhilarated and knowing look at each other, and then we came together in imperfect harmony...

"And IIIIIIII ye-iiiiiiiii will alwayyyyyyyyssss lurve yoooooo"

We collapsed back as the credits rolled, tears in our eyes and then laughter on our lips as we saw each other's reaction.

"Ugh, I love that movie."

Sarah gathered up the takeaway boxes, and I picked up the empty glasses and carried them into the kitchen. Just being next to her as I placed them down on the counter made my blood fizz. Some strange energy, like a magnetic force of nature that drew me to her. I don't know why I did it, I just *wanted* to. I put my hand softly on top of hers and our eyes darkened as we looked at each other.

Her lips were so perfect up close. I just wanted to taste them with my own, to feel her breath meet mine. Sarah looked up at me, wide-eyed and expectant, willing the moment onward. *God, when was the last time I had felt like this? Soft and vulnerable.* I took a chance and leaned in.

Sarah

My heart was pounding as he leaned in. My body desperate for him to kiss me and let my feelings fly. As his shadow covered me, I felt my insides flutter in anticipation. His hands gripped their way around me, holding me as a rush of wild excitement took me. Then, all of a sudden, the panic set in and I pulled my lips away from his.

He moved his head to try and meet me but I beat at his chest, his hands holding me so tightly I couldn't move them.

"Get off me! Let me go!"

"I'm not letting go," he said in an animal growl, "Until you kiss me."

I stopped trying to fight him. It was exhausting and pointless with his frame that was built for strength, his huge hands holding me like clamps, making me feel tiny as I looked up at the rush of thick hair across his chin. His piercing eyes stared down at me, wild and crazy with something... And that something was me.

Hayden leaned in again until his face was so close that it began to blur as his lips went in search of mine. His scent as he descended on me made me tremble, a deep animal musk that made me heady with excitement. His thick hands held me steady, my skin delighting at the touch and my body thankful for his grip, because otherwise I might have fallen under my weak legs. All I could see, all I could feel, all I could breathe, was *him*.

Inside, I melted. This was the moment I'd waited for, maybe all my life, but... The things he did, who he was... He couldn't be trusted. It was glaringly obvious that this would all end in heartbreak again, and I was sleepwalking right into it.

"Stop!" I commanded. Putting my hand with force against the steel of his chest. "No, Hayden, let me go."

He paused with confusion, before his forceful grip relaxed on my arms. I knew there would be bruises where his hands had held me so firmly. Delicious bruises that I would look at later and hate myself for this moment. *That was it, Sarah, that was your chance...*

We stared at each other, our eyes having their own private conversation, pleading with each other... *Do you mean it? You don't want... This?*

His gaze softened as he saw the decision had been made and was final, and the magic began to leave us. Hayden regained some of his composure before reluctantly releasing me. Then his eyes broke from mine and he sighed a long, slow, sad sigh that made me want to change my mind instantly, to soothe and heal him, to take him back to being wild and lost in the moment again.

Now it was just awkward. What words were there? There was nothing to be said that didn't sound uncomfortable.

Finally, feeling stupid and angry at myself, I rubbed my arms and blurted out, "I think you should go."

Hayden nodded without looking back up at me. Had I just broken this giant man's heart? Maybe just a little.

He stepped back, his vast shadow leaving me as I slipped off to the side, taking a last look at him before I turned and walked away from my dreams, angry tears rising in my eyes as I opened the door for him to leave.

20

DENIAL

Hayden

My insides hurt like hell, and it wasn't just the rosé. What was it with that woman? That quiet, sweet, pretty school teacher had somehow got under my armor—*me!* Hayden-*fucking*-Raynor!—and now it felt like I was falling apart.

"Hey, turn this up, would ya?" I told the Uber driver as Whitney came on the radio. I hummed along to *Somebody Who Loves Me* as the city lights faded behind us. *You really gotta get it together Hayden...*

Sarah

Alone again in my quiet apartment, all I felt was empty. My body had disappointment stretched across it. All that adrenaline and lust and desire that had sparkled between us. Wasn't that what I'd wanted? The truth is, I didn't know what I wanted anymore, but it wasn't this. All I had was a flat and sad emotion ringing through me.

I was mixed up and confused. Hayden wasn't a real

person. He was a fantasy. Just like Jake had been. Except, this time I could see what was coming.

I didn't want to be left with the aching feeling of just being another notch on a hockey player's bedpost, and at the same time, I didn't want to fall and find myself hurt and alone. Not again. That would be worse than just being alone. At least I didn't cry myself to sleep these days. Except, I could feel my eyes were wet already.

I didn't know what to do, but did I really think some big-shot professional hockey player was going to give me what I really craved, what I desired? The safety, love, and companionship that I needed over everything else. Outside, the rain began to patter harder on the windows.

Hayden

It took a half hour to get back home, and I'd just collapsed on the sofa when the doorbell rang.

Ignore it, ignore it! Then, after a beat, there was a heavy pounding on the door.

"Fuck," I breathed out, both annoyed at being disturbed and worried they'd wake Maiden.

With a scowl, I lifted my shadow off the sofa and went to see who in the hell was trying to get in. The intruder started banging again just as I flung the door open.

"Raynor! Oh, man, I'm so glad you're here!"

I stared back at Solly, stood there in my doorway. Looking down, I saw the duffle bag in his hand and knew this wouldn't be good.

"You gotta help me! Maria, she's lost it! Kicked me out, and she's on the warpath like you wouldn't believe. Screaming about divorce, taking the house! Going to the papers!"

His face was a picture of stress as I anxiously rubbed my neck and tried to figure out how to not tangle myself up in this mess.

"Jeez, Solly. Please, not now. You're a millionaire hockey player. Can't you go get a room at the Four Seasons or something? Or make a run for some Caribbean island and lie low?"

"There were photographers outside our house, Hayden! They know something and she's gonna *destroy* me! I can't be out there, they'll eat me up. Please!"

It was the same on the ice. Solly was skilled as heck, but he liked to show off about it, and as soon as some big guy who was missing a few teeth took exception to it and came at him, he was always looking to me to come and save him.

"Look Solly, I got Maiden, and now Cara is staying here," Solly pulled an awkward face when I mentioned Cara.

"I don't know where else to go right now," he said, his voice quiet and desperate.

"Fine!" I said. Not exactly enjoying the way *everyone* was walking all over me and treating my place as the hangout hotel right now, "Put your stuff in the playroom down the hall."

"Thanks so much, Hayden!" Solly said as he followed my outstretched arm down to Maiden's playroom. The thought of a 200 lb, six-foot-tall hockey player curled up in a sports car bed designed for a 6-year-old gave me a brief moment of pleasure.

Solly came back into the room as I slumped on the couch. "Got any beer, Hayden?"

"Beers are in the fridge, Solly."

"Okay, thanks man."

Solly opened two cold bottles and handed me one before joining me. I really didn't need this right now, but I knew Maria could be on the edge of crazy at the best of times.

"Okay, so what the fuck is going on here, Solly?"

"It was that *fucking* auction, Hayden... Beth Gibson. That tech tycoon's ex."

"Yeah, Rupert Hands' ex-wife, right? She's been hanging 'round the games this year."

"Right! Yeah, that's the one. She sponsors the fucking team's groin guards. Did you know that!?"

I laughed. I mean, hell, it was pretty funny.

"Maria was already hopping mad about me having to go for dinner with her, which is *ridiculous*. Hayden, you've seen her. She's not my type."

"She's not anyone's type," I agreed.

"Right? But Fletch said to keep her sweet, maybe even see if she wanted to throw around a bit more sponsorship money next year. So I played nice. I mean, I really tried to."

"You *tried* to?"

I took a long gulp of beer as I watched his face fall.

"We're in the ride over to the restaurant and she bangs on the limo window, tells the driver to go to this other address."

"Uh-oh."

"Yeah, and I'm like, *hey babe, where we going?* She puts her hand on my thigh and says *don't you worry about it...*"

I got myself a little comfier on the couch, wondering how bad this was going to get for poor Solly.

"...So now I *do* start worrying about it, Hay. I mean, she's all over me. I'm trying to keep it nice and in control, but she's like a wildcat."

"Solly, she's, what? A forty-five-year-old woman in a cardigan. You're a twenty-six-year-old 200 lb professional hockey player, are you joking?"

Solly blushed, then said weakly, "I was trying to keep her sweet Hayden. Like Fletch said."

"How sweet, Solly?"

"We get to the place and it's a hotel. I'm like, *there's no way I'm going in*, but she says, *I bought you for a hundred thousand dollars, so you better get in there*. What was I meant to do?"

"Please tell me you didn't…"

"No! …Well, not really. I mean, we just sort of fooled around in the room. Or rather, she fooled around while I tried to get out of there."

"Solly. Seriously."

"I only gave her enough to make it out of there alive without upsetting anyone. I didn't think anyone would find out!"

I wanted to open another beer, but I really didn't want to leave the story.

"So, how does Maria know all this?"

Solly looked at me with the face of someone who had just dropped their phone off the side of a boat while trying to take a picture of a fish.

"She… That woman…"

"Beth."

"Yeah, Beth. She told *everyone*, Hayden. Made it sound even worse than what really happened. Even my gardener knows about it! My *fucking* hairdresser was even looking at me funny. He definitely knows."

"Fun-time Solly." We both looked up to see Cara standing in the hallway, wearing a slinky silk gown on her body and a satisfied smirk on her face.

"Man chat Cara, take it somewhere else," I told her with contempt in my eyes.

Instead, she moved deeper into the room.

"Even I heard all about your little escapade, Solly, with those busy fingers of yours," she teased.

Solly went bright red.

"What... What did you hear exactly?" Then he looked nervously at me, not wanting to let the most embarrassing details make their way to my ears.

Cara smiled, she was enjoying this, "Oh, you little pervert. Every detail is already out there. The hockey bunnies are creaming themselves over it in the group chat."

Solly gulped, "They are?" Then he put his head in his hands, "Oh God, what am I gonna do?"

"I could help you if you want?" Cara said, and I glowered at her. This was how she set her traps. I'd seen it a million times, but once she'd made her web, there was no escape.

"You could? But how?"

"We just have to change the narrative, my dear Solly... Trust me, I'm better at spreading stories than she is."

It was true, Cara was able to make juicy gossip out of a french fry. I didn't like this for Solly though, not one bit.

"Cara, leave him alone," I said.

But Solly was looking at her, wide-eyed and desperate to be saved from his hell, ready to do anything. That's what gave me a feeling of dread.

21

NO SLEEP

Hayden

I couldn't sleep. I mean, how could I when there were Maiden's problems, that dumb incident outside the therapists, Cara spinning her webs, and now Solly? But none of that was what I was really thinking of. It was *her*.

That normal, nice school teacher. Maybe that was it, that she was *normal* and *nice*. There weren't many people like that in my world. It was more than that though, and I knew it. Something new was aching in me because of her.

Those lips like candy. The soft, warm skin that curved along her neck and stretched across her shoulders. Those green eyes that were so deep with intelligence, and a hint of sadness in them, that I just wanted to ease. Her scent, what was it? It slipped into my nose when we were close and I couldn't get it out of my head. It wasn't perfume. It was *her*. As if you could taste how sweet her body was in the air.

I dragged myself up and to the bathroom. There was no toilet paper in the en-suite and I suspected Cara had something to do with that. I trudged in the darkness down the hallway to the master bathroom. It wasn't entirely dark, though. There was a light on in the room at the end of the hall and faint sounds from Cara's room.

I padded quietly past the bathroom door and toward her room.

"...Yes, like that, exactly as I showed you... You make me happy, and I'll make it all go away..."

The door was slightly ajar, and I pushed it a crack wider with my fingertips. There was Cara, riding on top of Solly. Their naked bodies writhing on each other in the warm glow of the lamplight. I felt sick.

"Daddy?"

I turned and saw Maiden back down the hallway. He spoke sleepily as he rubbed his tired eyes. Marvin the dinosaur tugged tightly against his chest. Over their grunting, Solly and Cara didn't seem to notice, and I quietly padded my way back down the hallway to Maiden.

"You okay, Champ?" I kneeled down and asked in a whisper.

"What's mom doing?"

"Oh, don't worry about that. Silly grown-up stuff. Let's get you back to bed, okay?"

"I wasn't sleeping good, daddy."

"Huh, me neither. You wanna come crash with me tonight?"

Maiden nodded his sleepy head, and I felt a rush of fatherly love for that adorable little man. How had I bought all this into my home, *our* home?

"Okay, go get Pascal and we'll try get some sleep."

Pascal, a plush turtle we'd got at Six Flags five summers ago, had seen better days. I felt like that ragged plush turtle sometimes. Once shining, fun, and vibrant. Now it was ragged and battered by life, its eyes having been drawn back on with a marker pen more times than I could remember.

Like Pascal though, I would always be there for Maiden. He had me to rely on. *Who did I have, though?*

I scooped up Maiden, Marvin, and Pascal and carried them back to my bed, smiling at the tiny person in my arms, but also worried for him. When he was four, I'd lost him for a moment. Cara was supposed to be watching him while I swung by the bank, but being Cara, she'd got distracted by something shiny in a store. By the time I came back, he was gone. For the first time in my life, I froze. Incapacitated with absolute terror. Everyone had looked to me to act, but I didn't know what to do.

Twenty minutes later, we found him. Maiden had wandered into a kid's birthday party happening at the pizza joint next door. No one had noticed there was an extra kid, and he was happily chewing on a slice of pepperoni.

I'd never left him alone with Cara again. People couldn't be trusted. No one except me.

The rain began to beat down hard against the city that night as I lay restlessly, tussling with my aching feelings.

I couldn't risk it again, but maybe I had to. Something inside me was changing. The feelings I'd once shut down were operating again, compelling me to act. All I could think of was her. The soft curl of her brown hair caressing that smooth, exciting curve of her shoulder. Those slim, tiny wrists that made me crave to touch them. The sweet delight in her smile. And those eyes. Those fucking eyes that I wanted to fall into and never come back from. The way she squinted one of them when she laughed, the lines around her mouth that I wanted to press a thumb softly over. It felt almost irresistible. *Almost.*

My heart beat harder. It wasn't *almost*. It was true. I rolled out of bed, threw on a shirt, then stumbled out into the hallway and reached for my car keys.

22

THE RAIN

Sarah

The rain came down hard that night, driving its way into every available surface as if it had to get in somehow. I sat and watched it stream down the windows, blurring the city lights as I contemplated my life. I wanted love. I also wanted Hayden Raynor. But I couldn't see how those two things could come together. I wasn't some glamorous *It Girl* you chased. Women came to him, and I wasn't going to try and get my heart broken like that.

Hayden had been a fantasy, but now it was blurring into something else and I didn't know if I could handle it. I was shaken out of my thoughts by a thumping sound. The door pounding as if the person on the other side, like the rain, was desperate to get in.

It pounded again as I walked barefoot across the wooden boards, pausing to wonder what was lurking on the other side that was so mad to get inside.

Opening the door, there he stood. Looking at me like a hungry wolf, the rain streaking down his huge frame. There was nothing but fire in his eyes as he walked in without a word, striding toward me, dripping water across the floor as he came closer.

I tried to catch my breath as I stumbled backward, his eyes wild and intense. My ass bumped against the kitchen table and I was trapped there as he descended on me. Without hesitation, his mouth met mine, and I kissed him back hungrily. One big paw scooped me up by my ass and dropped me back down on the table. Our lips broke, and we looked deep into each other's vibrant, excited, and expectant eyes.

It seemed in that moment as if the world was electric. Everything melted away and there was only this.

"Lift up your skirt," he growled at me, raindrops pooling on the floor around my feet.

I gulped, my legs trembling as he looked down at me, a quivering rabbit cornered by a wolf, unable to resist the fate that was coming. There was no escape, and I craved it.

My fingers slipped down to my sides on his command. Slowly, I lifted up my dress, revealing the warm skin of my thighs and the soft white cotton panties underneath. His eyes left mine as he eagerly watched his prey being revealed to him, making me blush at the intensity of his look.

Hayden's other hand rose to my chest and pulled my dress open with one wild tug. My blood rushed with desire as he gently stroked the soft skin of my collarbone with his fingertips, admiring me.

His hand went lower, stroking my thighs, his fat thumb rising up between my legs and pressing down on my panties, my body softening at the touch.

As his lips came close to mine, I opened my mouth in expectation, but instead, his mouth slipped past me and went to the nape of my neck. His warm tongue tasted the salt from my warm skin as he ran one of his huge paws over me, trying to greedily touch all of me all at once. My nipples stiffened as he roughly pawed at my chest before pushing me down against the table. He lowered his head, the wet hair tickling my skin as his hot tongue traveled down my body, eagerly pulling me into his mouth.

Then all of a sudden, he scooped me up in those huge arms like I was weightless to him, and carried me toward my bedroom, kicking the door open like some kind of action movie star.

The mattress creaked in anguish under our weight as we fell onto the bed, the air rushing out of me underneath his huge frame as he fell on top of me, our lips feverishly kissing at each other, like it was our oxygen and we were desperately gasping for more of it.

I pulled with all my strength at his shirt, tearing it open, the pearl buttons scattering across the room and revealing his thick chest, my lips running kisses down him as he moaned in pleasure.

We were lost to each other as his hands slid under my dress and roughly pulled my panties from me, before he descended like a madman and his head fell between my quivering legs.

I was shaking with intense pleasure as his hot, wet tongue met me and took me deeper into a state of blissful, wild, arousal. Grasping tightly at his hair, I writhed under his thick tongue and moaned at the feel of his beard rasping against my thighs as I pulled him deeper.

He looked at me so intensely as he climbed back up my body to meet my eyes.

"Sarah... I need you."

"Uh-huh," was all I could reply, wide-eyed and helpless as he reared up and I pulled at his belt and pants. I couldn't wait, I was in an agonizing state that needed fulfilling right there and then.

Tearing down his shorts, I stopped, panting below him. He was so big. I looked up at him half-fearfully. The look he gave me back told me I had no choice. That huge, beautiful, throbbing monster was going to have me.

Then his hot breath was on my neck and I was howling in bliss... I was his now, all his, and there was no escape from it.

23

PANTING

Sarah

We lay side-by-side panting, a beautiful warm glow washing over me. It would have been perfect, if it hadn't been spliced with an agonizing feeling inside. A fantasy had walked out of my dreams and into my life. That in itself was a miracle that I would have been happy enough with, but now that it was over, it had to go back into my dreams again.

I looked over and Hayden smiled at me, his voice low and gentle as he spoke.

"I had to see you tonight."

"I'm glad you did Hayden." It was true, I was glad. But hell, I was also sad. Now that we'd stepped over that line and blurred fantasy with reality, it felt like an ending. It was done, and now we would return to where we belonged. Two worlds that shouldn't meet each other had done exactly that, for just a moment.

"Sorry," he sighed, rolling onto his back, "But I do have to go soon. I need to be there for Maiden when he wakes up."

I reached out and stroked my fingertips across his shoulder, the skin warm and smooth, stretched tightly over his rigid collarbone.

"I know Hayden. This was nice. But I know. Now we can go back to where we're supposed to be."

"Maybe this is where we're supposed to be?"

"We both know it's not. You want to protect yourself, but you have to understand that I do, too. I can't let myself be ruined again. It's not fair to do that."

Hayden sighed again and rolled back to face me, my side of the bed lifting me up under his weight as he did so, "Whatever he did to you, I'm not him."

"Hayden, you know this isn't real. You're not real. You're a fantasy to me. Perhaps I'm even the same for you."

"I'm real," he told me, putting my hand on his chest, right where his heart was beating. "Let me change your mind."

I wavered, wanting to believe him, but how could I? He belonged with people who would fit right into his world. I would be the odd fish in a sea of beautiful mermaids, until it was so clear that I would be left again. Thrown back to my ocean of bottom feeders with only regrets.

"I think you should go, Hayden. Not in a bad way. I just think we should leave this as a beautiful moment, and that's where it stays."

24

CRACKING

Hayden

Goddamnit. She was right. *Wasn't she?* But then why did it feel so wrong?

Four years of turning my head away from every girl who threw themselves in front of me and then, when I finally break my own rules, finally let go and throw myself at someone, they turn me away.

Maybe those bunnies and influencers and starry-eyed girls were all I deserved. Someone normal didn't want to be a part of what I was. Why would they? I was just a fantasy. A face from a magazine or on the television, not an actual person. Certainly not the guy who took the trash out, went to bake sales, or wanted to hang out watching old movies all weekend.

But the thing is, that's what I'd rather be doing most of the time. Except that I was good at one thing. Hockey. Okay, two things. Hockey and fighting. Maybe three, if you include karaoke.

It's not like I could walk in tomorrow, quit the team, then

go back to live like that. *Or could I?* No. I had Maiden to look out for. It was funny to think that Sarah had been looking out for him too. No one had asked her to. She wanted to. Because she was nice and kind and beautiful and—*oh my God*—I'm a fucking mess!

My chest sunk as I remembered her eyes earlier, the way she looked at me. Two sparkling emerald pearls that spoke to me in ways I have never been spoken to before. How warm her skin was, the fizz of excitement when she ran her fingertips along my collarbone, her tiny pretty wrists, that intoxicating scent that I couldn't help closing my eyes to savor the memory of.

My shell was cracking. I'd spent so long alone that I really believed I didn't need anyone else. But now, I wasn't so sure. What I'd thought and how I felt were at odds. Everything I'd given to Maiden - safety, warmth, love - I'd forgotten to give myself. I'd put it all out of mind. For once, I'd gotten to feel all of those things, a glimpse of what that would be like. But, like it had always been, it was taken away from me. Maybe I truly was unloveable, but for once, couldn't it stay, if only for a little longer?

25

AN INVITE

Sarah

It might have been the right thing to do, but there really was no getting rid of him.

"Hey there," he said, looking absolutely gorgeous in his shades, tight jeans stretched around tree trunk legs, a pristine white t-shirt, and an open button-up shirt flowing around him in the sunlight.

I blushed and smiled back uncomfortably, crossing my arms across my chest.

"Hi," Maiden waved at me cheerfully.

I smiled at him as he ran off into the classroom with Marvin and went straight up to Matthew Locklear. It was heartwarming to see how they'd become friends now.

"So... Um, about last night..." It was strange seeing such a big intimidating man looking so worried about choosing his words.

"It's okay Hayden, we had a few drinks and got a bit carried away. You don't have to explain. I mean The Bodyguard does things to people."

He smiled at that, but in a sad kind of way. Those big eyes looked so real. I wanted him to be real, but he couldn't be.

When there were no more words from either of us, he frowned and said, "Okay, sure."

He turned to leave and then stopped, looking back to tell me, "Sarah, it's a great movie, and the wine was nice and all, but I don't think that's what last night was about."

His face was deeply serious and there was something new and intense in his look, a longing maybe?

"It was nice Hayden, we can leave it at that."

"Orrr..." His eyebrow climbed up his forehead as he dragged out the sound.

I looked back at him, narrowing my eyes and trying to read what he was about to say. "Or?"

"Crazy thought. I could use a date for this thing on Wednesday."

Was he serious? Hayden Raynor, the man who didn't date, was asking *me* on a date.

It was ludicrous, but I couldn't stop myself from asking, "What thing?"

"It's like a Mayor's Ball thing, probably a bit stuffy. I don't know if it's your thing." He stroked the back of his neck and looked up at me nervously.

I half-scoffed. It had to be a joke. It was the socialite soiree of the year, the kind that you looked at all the photos of the next day to see who wore what.

"You mean *the* Mayor's Ball!"

"Uh, yeah. I think there's only one Mayor," he said, before adding, "Oh, there's free drinks!"

"Hayden, I know what the Mayor's Ball is!"

"Oh, so what do you think?"

I'd made my mind up already. This was going too far,

getting too deep. I could only see myself being embarrassed, abandoned, and probably humiliated again if I let myself do this.

"Um, I'm sorry, Hayden. I can't do Wednesday."

"Gotcha," he said sadly, trying to sound as if he wasn't disappointed. Was he *actually* disappointed? "Well, hey, see you around then, Sarah."

"Yeah. See you around Hayden."

And with that, he turned on his heels as the school bell rang out. He went back to his glamorous life, and I went back to my... Life.

"You did what!?"

Kensy and I had holed up at Denny's after work. I'd have preferred cocktails, but at least the coffee was good, and their lava cake was a dream.

"C'mon Kensy. He's a fantasy. It's not real. Let's not forget the two dates before that."

"Hayden *fucking* Raynor threw himself at you and you, YOU, turned him out."

Kensy was staring at me with shocked bemusement. "What did he say?"

"Oh. Well," I avoided Kensy's eyes, "This morning he invited me to the Mayor's Ball, if you can believe that!"

I thought for a moment she was going to faint, "The Mayors... OH MY GOD!"

"I mean, I said no."

"You said... No!?"

"Well, it is quiz night," I added weakly, knowing how poor that sounded.

"QUIZ NIGHT! ...Okay. What the hell, Sarah!"

I stared back at her, shrugged my shoulders, and pulled a face that said *what-ya-gonna-do?*

Kensy looked at me furiously. I'd never seen her look like this. I mean, I'd seen her doing her stern teacher act when faced with boisterous kids, but this was something else. It was actually pretty intimidating. I wondered if she was about to punch me square in the face in sheer rage.

As I stared helplessly at her, she took a long sigh, preparing herself to say the next words.

"Sarah. Look. I can handle this. The school, Hicks, the teacher-parent evenings, *quiz night*. I fit here. This is my happy. But I've known you for five years now and I keep waiting - waiting and goddamn *hoping* - for the day that you finally tell me you're leaving."

I watched her, frowning.

"This," and she signaled to the room we were in, "This is not where your story ends, Sarah, we both know it. You want more than this, you deserve more than this, and I know you know it," she leaned in and eyeballed me, "Stop worrying about falling and go and fucking jump."

Fuck. I didn't like being told off. I also hated that Kensy might be right.

When I'd come back to Merryville, I didn't know how I would ever move forward. Happiness and love was the last thing on my mind. It was just *how can I stop feeling so bloody miserable?* And the only answer I could find that worked was to just turn it all off. To reject love. All those feelings and hopes. Those silly girlish dreams. It all got locked away.

I was so convinced that I didn't deserve anything else that I just gave up and settled for the easy option, because it didn't come packaged up with all that potential for being hurt again. I'd felt so weak and vulnerable that I couldn't even face the idea of it. Then I simply forgot what else there was. It was just easier to be alone.

Kensy put her hand on mine and stared at me intensely. "I'm serious Sarah, you can't pass this up. Do you really not want to find out?"

I looked back at her doubtfully, playing with the chocolaty crumbs on the plate in front of me.

"I mean, *maybe*?"

"Sarah, for the love of God! Go and get him!"

The violence of her words shook me up. Feelings in me that had been long buried were unceremoniously dug up and emerged from dark, hidden corners. For the first time in years, I felt the vague possibility of the chains loosening around my trapped heart. The person I'd once loved being, who was once so hopeful and excited for love, she was still there, waiting behind the mask I'd hidden her under.

It wouldn't be all that easy, but letting myself feel free of the sadness and letting in some hope for just a moment, was a breath of fresh air. Of course, it also came loaded with the horrifying idea that the fresh air might just as easily be poisonous and deadly and choke me.

Kensy saw my expression change as the realization slowly dawned on me.

"We'll take my car!" She said with a burst of excitement.

There was a moment as we looked at each other, making sure we were both on the same page. Then we jumped to our feet.

Out on the highway, my stomach felt sick. Not because of what I was about to do, but because Kensy was swerving like a maniac through traffic, like we were racing toward the emergency room.

"Kensy, slow down! Jeez!"

The excitement might have got the better of her, but I was still unsure about all this.

"I don't know, Kensy," I really didn't. I felt sick with nerves. "I can just text him."

"No! You gotta do it face to face." She yelled as she careered between cars again, smashing her horn at them.

Yeah, if we even make it there, I thought.

Hayden

I put the car in drive and took off for Tommy's. A cold beer and a dark spot were exactly what I needed right now. Anything but pining and feeling like this. I didn't take rejection well, but Sarah had made it perfectly clear how she felt, and *fuck*, if it didn't hurt like hell. That woman had wounded me and, as much as I tried to put it out of my mind, I couldn't.

Jimmy was already there, lounging in a booth and leafing through the sports section of the paper.

"Hayden, you look like shit."

"Yeah, well, at least I don't smell like it."

"Except, you do."

We slapped each other on the back with a grin and I eyed the half-empty pitcher of beer waiting on the table. "Couldn't wait, huh?"

Jimmy sighed as he sat back down - One of those long, *fuck my life* kind of sighs - and I filled a glass for myself.

"I'm tired, Hay," he told me, rubbing his face. "I hardly see my kids or Gina, and the attitude on these young wannabe stars, they think they know it all. Like, they tell *me* what to do! Used to be the other way round, but no one listens anymore."

"Like this kid," he stabbed his finger at a photo in the paper of Logan Hunter, America's latest loud-mouthed track athlete, "We're in a meeting with K-Sports, and I swear to God, right in the middle of it, he turns to me and tells me to go get him a cup of coffee."

"Damn Jimmy, I'm sorry, that sounds rough. Hey, you ever want to get out and come to Merryville, maybe open an antiques store, do some fishing, eat and drink ourselves fat, I'm right behind you."

"Few more years to go yet. Then I'm out, Hay."

"Same for me Jimmy, except I don't think I have much choice in the matter. It gets harder every year."

"You remember in college, that girl, Betty?"

"Bet-sy," I corrected him, while nodding as the memory flooded back.

"Yeah, she was sweet on you, and you sent her my way."

"Yup, got bored with giving her the pork sandwich and needed somewhere else for her to go."

"You... What?" Jimmy looked incredulous.

"Relax, I'm fucking kidding Jimmy! Never touched the girl. I swear I didn't."

"Uh-huh. 'Course you didn't!" He laughed. "Sometimes I think that maybe if I'd got with Betsy and taken a job in her dad's hardware store, all this would be different."

"You know she's in jail, right?"

"Really? I did not know that."

"Tried to stab her husband with a screwdriver, if I recall rightly."

Jimmy's eyes got wider. "Huh, guess it ain't so bad then."

We both took a moment to think about Betsy and being on the end of that screwdriver, before Jimmy got to what he really wanted to know about.

"So, you gonna tell me what all that was about last night?"

"Ah, Jimmy, I would, but it's nothing. Didn't really pan out."

"You gotta be careful mixing with the locals, Hay. Before you know it, they're a bleeding heart telling every news station and glossy magazine in town their story."

"This one's not like that."

Jimmy looked at me, trying to read my expression. If anyone knew me, it was this guy. He could've laughed at me, called me out, but he could tell it was a sensitive topic and to respect it.

"So, you like this one, huh?"

"I don't know Jimmy. It doesn't matter anyway, she's not interested, and…"

Jimmy said it for me, "I don't date."

"Exactly," I nodded at him.

We sipped our beers for a reflective moment before Jimmy spoke again.

"Hay, I've never seen you give up on anything in your life, even when it got real goddamn hard. Nothing, except for one thing."

I looked at him doubtfully. *Was everyone my fucking shrink these days?*

"Please don't tell me you're about to say *love*, Jimmy?"

He smiled into his glass, gently nodding, and I groaned and rolled my eyes.

"Hay. You can pretend it doesn't matter, but one look at you and I can see it does. You got the bug. It's in your eyes."

Normally, I'd shut it down, make a joke, and move things along. Thing is, Jimmy always had a way of getting people to say what he somehow already knew. He could just read people like that.

"Okay, cards on the table."

"Deal me in."

"It's Maiden's teacher." I waited for a reaction, but Jimmy's eyebrows only lifted a little and he waited patiently for me to continue.

"Sarah. I don't remember meeting anyone like that. I mean, she's not like anyone else. She's kind, even when she's mad at me, and I've done that to her enough. Even then, I just love her looking at me... Usually, it's just animal attraction, but with her... It's... It's like I just want to scoop her up and make her safe and warm and happy."

"And that would make you happy?"

"Feels like it. But then again, my feelings go all batshit crazy around her. I keep fucking it up and I hate myself for it, but..."

"Hay, from experience, you and self-sabotaging *anyone* who gets close to you is pretty standard."

He was right of course, but it still felt bad to hear.

"Hayden!"

I turned in the direction that my name came from and saw a girl approaching.

"Er, yeah, hi there."

"It's Kelly! We were at Worship together the other night." Then to illustrate further, she rolled out her tongue, crossing her eyes at the same time in a cartoonish way.

Ah yes, the girl with the tongue piercing. Was she following me?

"Cool. So Kelsy..."

"Kelly," she corrected me.

"Got it. I'm just catching up with my agent here."

"Oh, okay! Just wanted to say hi. Hey, let's take a selfie!"

"Nah, I think..."

But she was already draped across me with her phone held out and giggling. "Say *peaches*!"

I gave a weak half-smile as she threw up the obligatory selfie fingers.

"Thanks. Hey, you wanna go to Inferno tonight? It's going to be *wild*!"

"Nope. Can't tonight, sorry."

"Aw," she pouted, then her wide not-a-care-in-the-world smile came back, like it was on a rubber band. "Well, see you around then!"

"Jeez," Jimmy said as she walked away, tapping on her phone.

"Yeah, I don't know where they get their weird energy from, honestly."

"So, what?" Jimmy wasn't about to let me off the hook. "You ask her out again? The teacher?"

"Actually, I kind of asked her to the Mayor's Ball, but she said no."

"Oh," a serious expression darkened on Jimmy's face. "Hayden, that's probably for the best."

Now it was my turn to raise my eyebrows at him.

"Cara's already been on the phone with me about that."

Goddamnit, Cara couldn't keep her fingers out of anything.

"And what does Cara want now, Jimmy?" My head was beginning to throb.

"Hay, you think she just happened to be in town at the same time? That woman's always got an agenda. She's got some bespoke Marc Jacobs dress that apparently, I have to pick up for her. She's expecting to go with you."

Or if not me, then Solly, I thought. *So that was her game.*

"What's that look, Hay? I get you don't like it, but you know Cara."

"Jimmy, I gotta tell you. Solly's been staying at mine after another drama with Maria. Also, him and Cara hooked up."

"Oh hell, no!"

"Yeah. I don't like it either."

"Hay, Maria can be a nightmare, but she's a good lady. They'll figure it out. She's not going to shut out the father of her kids. Then again, she is one hell of a jealous woman, so if *that* comes out..."

Jimmy pulled an uncomfortable face.

"Uh-huh. So I don't really have a choice, do I? Cara gets her designer dress to show off at the ball, Solly gets off the hook, and I have to play nice so those two can be happy."

"Sorry Hay. Sometimes you don't see the play until it's too late."

Sarah

As Kensy pulled up outside Hayden's place, I had a newly found energy bubbling inside me. I thought I'd be anxious as hell, and I was after Kensy's unsettling driving, but not about this.

She was right. He'd already asked me. All I had to do was walk up to the door and tell him, *Hayden, forget what I said. I want to come with you. Take me to the ball.* My heart danced a little just at the thought of what that might be like, all dressed up and out at an exclusive soiree with the captain of the Ice-Hawks on my arm.

"You ready?" Kensy asked.

"I'm ready, Kensy. Thank you. For everything." We hugged each other, and she gave me a sweet, encouraging smile.

It felt like a long walk up to Hayden's door, the seconds somehow stretching into an eternity, my legs feeling heavier with every step. *Keep your cool Sarah, this is going to be a good moment.* When I finally got there, I took a deep breath to compose myself, shook my hair out, rang the doorbell, and then looked down.

Oh, what the hell was I wearing? In all the excitement, I hadn't even thought about it. I looked like I'd just stepped out of a secretarial college in the 80s. I quickly removed my glasses as I heard someone coming.

The door opened. But, instead of his looming figure appearing, two pale blue eyes stared out at me. And they looked annoyed.

"Er, yeah. Can I help you?"

I knew Cara from her photos, but up close she was something else, wearing a short blue-gray silk gown with embroidered dragons, showing off her perfectly toned and tanned legs. Damn, she was pretty. I felt ridiculous in comparison. How could I compare to a creature like that?

"Well?"

"Oh," I stumbled, losing some of my nerve under her fierce gaze, "Well... Um... Is Hayden home?"

"What are you, a reporter?" She scowled at me and started to close the door.

"Oh, no, no! I'm Maiden's teacher."

"Huh. Is that right?" Then she hollered over her shoulder, "MAIDEN!"

Quiet footsteps padded over to the door and Maiden peeked his head out.

"Is this your teacher?"

He looked afraid of her. *That made two of us.* Maiden smiled at me, then it slipped from his face as he turned back to Cara and nodded, before running off.

"Okay. What is it then?"

"Oh, I just wanted to talk to Hayden for a moment."

"He's not here. If it's about Maiden, you can just tell me."

"No, it's about Wednesday, I just... Well, I'll come back, maybe."

"Wednesday," she thinned her eyes at me. "You mean the ball? What are you babysitting or something?"

"No... I mean, he invited me and I just wanted to tell him..."

She laughed cruelly.

"Yeah. I don't know what you *think* is happening, but Hayden has a date for the ball. Me. It's not for..." She looked me up and down. "Well, people like you. What would you even wear? Something from Sears!?"

Her lips were thick with a sickly mocking smile, as if I disgusted her.

In return, I just stood there with my mouth flapping like a salmon out of water.

"Okay then. Good chat. BYE!" she said when I didn't speak. Then the door was unceremoniously closed on me as I stood there frozen, red-faced, and embarrassed.

As I trudged back to the car, my expression told Kensy everything.

"I guess that didn't go... well?" Kensy asked.

My phone pinged. It was Bernard.

Haven't heard from you in a while. Dinner at mine later?

"Let's just get out of here, Kensy," I told her.

As I unlocked my phone, Hayden's Instagram flashed up. There was a newly tagged post from @*hotttbunnygirl*, the two of them grinning as she splayed across his knee in a bar. Below was the comment *Love my Hellraiser*, followed by several skulls, aubergines, and fire engine emojis. Whatever picture they were painting, it made my mood darken even more.

I'd let myself get carried away, and I hated myself for it. I didn't fit into this world of glamorous influencers, models, and bunnies. I barely even fit into my own world of grubby kids, sad teachers, and cheap wine. Hell, I was the kind of person who couldn't even afford a car, having my best friend driving me around instead.

My sadness turned into annoyance, then to anger, which quickly gathered pace as I let my feelings bubble up. Since Hayden Raynor had arrived in my life, things had been getting worse and worse. I had to let it go, before I spiraled any further into my own personal quagmire.

26

CLEANING HOUSE

Hayden

Goddamn Cara! I was sick of her coming in and messing up everyone's lives. To hell with it. She had to go. For me, for Maiden, for Solly, and whoever else was caught up in her twisted shit.

As I slammed the front door and threw my keys on the table, she came drifting into the lounge in her silk gown like some kind of sexy ghost, accessorized with a martini in her hand.

"Oh, well, hey there, Hay-Ray."

I scowled back at her.

"Cara, I need you to get your annoying ass out of here."

"Aw, you used to like my annoying ass Hay Ray," she pouted back at me with a soft, seductive lisp.

Jesus. She thought she could seduce her way out of anything. Not that she was wrong, exactly. There'd been enough times when I was completely done with her and she had lured me into bed. That spell had gone a long time ago, though. Now she'd lost that power over me, she just threatened me with losing Maiden, or the house, or creating one of her tornados of gossip. It didn't matter to her if any of it was true or not. As long as she got what she wanted, and I was just another worm on her hook.

"I'm not kidding Cara."

Her expression shifted to one that said she was bored with this and wasn't interested in playing this game. "Oh, don't be so serious Hayden. I'll be out of your hair in a day or two."

"No," I told her, defiantly.

In return, she laughed at me, making me even more angry.

"Hay-Ray, here's the thing," she slinked up to me and put her fingertips on my chest, looking up into my eyes. "You're a *fucking* coward."

I stared back at her, gritting my teeth, deciding whether or not to just pick her up and throw her out through the window.

"It's been seven years since I walked out on you. Aside from Maiden, and whatever's going on with that Joyce woman, I'm still the only person you can feel anything for. You know why?"

My eyes thinned in simmering contempt at that awful woman. Her eyes were shining back at me, enjoying inflicting her little piece of torture on me. "Because the big scary hellraiser is just a scared little boy."

"Get out!" I yelled, pointing to the door, but she just kept looking at me with the acrid smell of vodka on her breath.

"Look. I'm selfish and mean and I get what I want, Hayden, but at least I'm honest about it. You're hiding in this little fortress you've built, telling everyone you're protecting your kid, but really you're trapped in here with no one but yourself."

I sighed wearily. I didn't need a lecture from Cara, of all people. She knew exactly what to say to twist the knife deep into you. Perhaps in some ways, she was right, though.

"All that bravado and you can't even be brave enough to let anyone near you. Like that teacher you seem so obsessed with." I blushed and gave her a dirty look. She really knew how to get under my skin, but how did she know about Sarah?

"Oh Hay-Ray, look at you," she started playing with my collar, like a fussy mother. "Take some advice, even though you don't want it. Let yourself be happy."

Then, unexpectedly, Cara put her arms around me and hugged me. For once, it didn't seem like a ploy, but an actual real human interaction. Not that you could tell either way with Cara.

She spoke softly into my chest, "Show Maiden what that is. What letting someone in can be like. It's better than hiding him and you away in here. He needs to know Hayden. I can't be his mother. I don't have it in me, and you can't know how much that hurts. Seeing you being all dad-like, and knowing I don't have that in me. But that doesn't mean that he doesn't deserve it."

"You still need to leave Cara."

"Tomorrow. After the ball." She said, putting her head on my chest and tapping my shoulders as I sighed. "One last night and then I'm gone."

27

CHANGING

Sarah

I skipped quiz night. I didn't want to be out and around people. Not normal people, not kids, not mountain-sized hockey players, not the fancy crowd at that dumb Mayor's Ball, none of them. Kensy, I could make an exception for. Also, she bought over wine, face and hair masks, and Ooey-Gooey ice cream, so I was happy to let her in.

We both sighed happily in our dressing gowns as we lay back, Say Anything playing on the TV.

I raised my glass. "Fuck men."

"And ...," Kensy added, as we clinked glasses. "If we're going to be girls in our dressing gowns, eating ice cream, drinking wine, smelling *amazing*, and watching rom-coms for the rest of our lives, then so be it. I'm good with that.

"Scrubbing men's shirts, collecting their beer bottles, listening to their snoring, having to hear every sports game that's ever played on the television at full blast, bearing their children... Love sucks!"

John Cusack was just about to hold up his boombox in the rain when a rapping came from the door.

"Pizza!" Kensy and I squealed at the same time.

I pulled the cucumber pieces off my eyes, but didn't bother to remove the face mask. It was highly unlikely John Cusack worked as a delivery driver for Go-Go Pizza these days. Although I couldn't be entirely sure about that, it was a risk I was willing to take.

Opening the door, I looked with confusion at the suited man in my doorway, who in turn paused with fright when he saw the masked, frazzle-haired woman before him.

"Hi. Erm, Sarah?"

I stared back blankly at him, looking down at his hands and wondering why he wasn't holding two boxes full of oozing mozzarella-drenched pepperoni with extra banana peppers and the grease leaking through their cardboard containers. When I looked back up at him, he was still waiting for me to respond.

"Yes... Who are you?" I replied a bit snappily, starting to feel angry that my evening in was being disturbed by anything other than hot gushy pizza.

His eyes sparkled as he spoke. "I'm Jimmy. You ready to go to the ball tonight?"

Kensy yelled from the couch, "Make sure they didn't forget the butter-garlic sauce this time!"

I stood bewildered, "The... Wait. What now?

"The Mayor's Ball, you got an hour, and I got a dress in the car for you."

"Sorry, who are you?"

"Jimmy. Hayden's agent."

I groaned in reply.

"Look. He didn't send me. But, trust me, he wants you

there, even if he doesn't know it. So, you'll be my date for tonight if you'll have me."

Kensy came over to see what all the fuss was with the pizza man. Standing there in our ghoulish masks peering at the man, he turned and walked back to his car, opened the trunk, and came back holding a gown covered in a plastic protector.

"What's going on Sarah? That doesn't look like pizza," she whispered to me.

"I don't know exactly. But, apparently, this man is here to take me to the Mayor's Ball."

"The Mayor's..." Kensy stumbled on the words as Jimmy came back to the door.

"It's an Oscar de la Renta. The woman who was supposed to wear it just went to rehab - slightly unwillingly and at the last minute - but it still turned up. I think it's a close fit."

Kensy repeated his words in a dreamy-sounding voice, "Oscar de la Renta..."

"Okayyy then," I said to him suspiciously, taking the dress from his hands in a daze as Kensy rocked on her heels next to me.

I turned, closed the door, and we looked at each other in disbelief. Then the screaming started. Was this actually happening? It was straight out of a fairytale.

The next hour was a blur of wild and fantastic energy. Kensy and I feverishly emptying make-up bags into piles, washing, blow-drying, straightening, preening. We did and redid my eye make-up at least four times.

"Kensy..."

"Uh uh!" She shut me down as she finished delicately lifting my lashes. "Stop thinking! Just turn it off and go have the evening of your life. I swear, Sarah, I'll be mad as hell if you mess this up."

"Okay. Thanks, Kensy," I told her affectionately. "What's he doing now?"

Kensy went and pulled back the curtain as I slipped into the dress. The softest satin and lace pressed against my skin like a sensual love letter. The shimmering cracked effect of the pattern seemed to come alive in the light as the blanket of perfect joy gently bobbed around my ankles. *I can't believe this fits,* I whispered to myself in disbelief.

"He's still just sat in his car waiting. I think he might be air-drumming."

She turned back to me and gasped, "Are. You. Fucking. Kidding me!"

I looked over to the full-length mirror and my hand rose to my mouth. There was no denying it. I looked fucking incredible. I mean, I glowed in that dress. This must be what superheroes feel like when they put on their costumes. Suddenly pulled out of being dull and ordinary and changed into something amazing. I couldn't remember the last time I'd looked or felt remotely like this.

"No, no!" Kensy cried out as the tears came to my eyes, "The make-up!"

She held up her handkerchief and gently dabbed at my wet eyes.

"Hey," she stood back, her mouth hanging open. "My God. You look absolutely stunning, Sarah."

Then it was Kensy's turn to dab at her eyes.

"Well, I guess I'm ready then."

"More than ready," she said, admiring me so intensely

that I couldn't help but blush in delight at her dazzled attention.

I stepped outside and my mystery date quickly hopped out of the car and walked round to open the passenger door for me with a surprised and pleased look on his face.

"You look fabulous, Sarah," he told me softly as he approached. The look in his eyes told me he meant it, too.

28

BALLED OUT

Sarah

I liked Jimmy immediately. For a start, he immediately switched the radio over from Classic Rock Hits, and Taylor Swift's 'Change' came on the airwaves. It made me smile as we cruised through my neighborhood and toward the twinkling city lights. All those homes we passed were full of people who would never know what it felt like to be wearing a high-end designer dress on a soft luxury leather seat, on their way to mix with the rich and famous. I tried to forget for a moment that I was one of those people too, because tonight that was exactly what I was doing.

The real nerves didn't come until we reached the city. Through the tinted windows, I could hear the swell of buzz and excitement from the crowd who had come out to catch a glimpse of those attending the ball. All hoping that some of their stardust might rub off on them and they would be sucked into that vibrant other world that ran parallel with theirs. I, however, was a complete imposter. An infiltrator.

Snuck in the backdoor by some strange twist of fate that I didn't entirely understand.

"Hey. So, that's Farla Robinson's car in front of us," Jimmy told me.

I gasped. I'd seen her on billboards all over the city. She was like a goddess in Merryville.

"You know she grew up in a trailer park in Southview? Still gets her security team to pick her up KFC."

"For real?"

"That's right. Don't be intimidated by these people Sarah, they're not everything you think they are, believe me."

I nodded, thankful for the reassurance. But the butterflies flooded my stomach again as Jimmy flashed his pass through the window at the security, and then we pulled up to the concierge at the bottom of the red carpet.

"What if someone asks me who I am, Jimmy?"

"Just tell them you do charitable work for vulnerable children in the city. It's *almost* true and no one's going to push you on that."

Then the car door opened and the noise and cameras blinded me, all clamoring to catch whoever was about to step out, desperate to capture them as a still image that could be looked at and commented on by people all over the world. The flashes quickly slowed as they realized I was no one worthy of their efforts.

Stood there awkwardly at the bottom of the carpet, holding my hands over my dazed eyes, the lights still burned onto my retinas, Jimmy came beside me. He took my arm and led me, blinking heavily, between the crowd and across the thick red velvet carpet toward the entrance to the ball.

A few more flashes went off and someone yelled at me, "Hey! Beautiful dress!"

I turned to see where the voice came from and the yeller lifted his camera to his eye.

"Why don't you show it off?" Jimmy said in my ear, followed by an encouraging wink.

I remembered how I'd looked in the mirror before I left and a burst of sweet confidence flooded through me. Hell, I might as well make the most of this. Who knows if I would ever look this good again? I made a couple of (at least what I thought was) glamorous poses and suddenly felt the rush of being on the other side of the camera, on the other side of life, and I *liked* it. Then the next car pulled up, and suddenly all the attention was ripped away from me and passed onto the new arrival. I suppose that's fame in a nutshell.

We entered the reception, and I clung tighter to Jimmy's arm, feeling increasingly like a fraud.

"Hey, can I leave you a second? I've got to shake some hands, but I'll be back," Jimmy said.

He saw my horrified expression and looked around the room.

"Hmm. Okay, let me introduce you to Andrea Barker over there. She's kind of snooty, but you'll be safe with her for a moment."

Andrea Barker looked like a Disney villain with silver streaks running through her dark hair, but I nodded anyway and Jimmy led me over.

"Andrea, my dear. Please meet Sarah... Erm..." Jimmy turned to me to fill in the missing pieces.

"Sarah Miller! Very nice to meet you, Miss Barker."

Andrea looked down her nose at me, sighed, and then said witheringly, "Yes, it must be nice for you, I suppose."

Jimmy spun to smoothly lift two glasses of champagne

Hockey Heart

off a tray from a passing waiter and handed one to me. "I'll be back in a moment, okay?"

I nodded and looked back at my new and reluctant babysitter.

"So, Miller. What is it you do? Please don't say *influencer* or I might choke."

"Oh. No, I work with privileged children in the city."

"Privileged children?" She replied with a frown.

My face reddened at the mistake and I stumbled back at her, "Oh, I mean they weren't privileged, but now they are."

"Oh, right. I see," she said, still unsure, before adding, "But... Why?"

"You mean... Why work with children?"

"That's exactly what I mean."

Jimmy arrived back just in time to rescue me.

"Andrea, I hope you're playing nice," he smiled at her knowingly.

"*Nice* is not me Mr. Kemp, I prefer *elegant*," then she flashed another look at me, "Absolutely gorgeous dress, by the way."

Jimmy gave a wide smile in return and, to my relief, led me away.

"You're sure getting some attention in that outfit, my dear," he whispered to me, a warm glow lighting up inside my chest at the recognition.

As we walked through the crowd, I noticed the beautiful woman we'd seen at the auction. She was talking to Solly Ricek with a stern look on her face. I wondered how his date with the cardigan had gone on that same evening I'd spent with Hayden.

The walk through to the main hall took some time. Jimmy had to stop every few steps to shake hands, bearhug, fist-bump, and backslap all kinds of people, none of whom paid me any attention to me beyond a quick glance. It suited me, though. I wasn't sure I could hold a conversation with some of these types. It was all names and faces, that's all they seemed to be interested in.

Finally, we made it through the reception and into the main hall. Smart-suited men and glamorous women - all adorned in the finest clothes, jewelry, and accessories - milled around large circular tables beneath a grand array of chandeliers. Each table was dressed in a perfectly white tablecloth, marked in a flourish with flowers of violet, white, and rusted red, gleaming glasses, and champagne buckets. In one warmly lit corner, a soft jazz band added a glamorous touch to the surroundings.

We were guided to our table and my heart froze. There was Hayden and, *Goddamnit*, he looked stunning in his tailored dark suit, fresh white shirt, and impeccable bowtie.

Lounging back in his chair, he was talking and laughing over his shoulder to a group at another table and didn't see us approach. Those pale blue eyes I had encountered only yesterday did see us, though, and Cara seemed to glower with disgust as we came closer. As she looked me up and down in my picture-perfect dress, her look only became darker and more sinister.

"Cara, good to see you," Jimmy said, and I sensed the hint of falseness around his words as Cara stood, holding her Dolce clutch, and air-kissed both his cheeks. She stared cold-heartedly and directly at me, and my heart jumped again, this time with uneasy fear.

"Oh. *The teacher*," she said, flatly and unimpressed. "I didn't realize it was *that* kind of charity function."

Jimmy looked at me uncomfortably before Hayden turned back to the table, grinning. When he saw me, his eyes widened. He didn't speak, but he just gawped at me, taking in the glamorous woman stood before him. He knew me, but he didn't know *this* me.

"Sarah?" He finally managed, as I blushed in delight at his reaction, pleased at how I'd caught his attention. *Yeah, I know Hayden, I look fucking great, don't I?*

"Oh. Hi, Hayden," I said with a soft smile.

His eyes swung to Jimmy with a crinkle on his forehead, asking the question his lips didn't need to.

"Hope you don't mind that I brought a date, Hay?" Jimmy said, a mischievous gleam sparkling in his eyes.

Hayden bounced to his feet and came to pull my chair out for me. *This was already an improvement on last time.* I could smell the cologne on his collar, like a forest on a sparkling spring morning, all bark, musk, lush moss, and dew.

Cara folded her arms as she watched us, rolled her eyes, and then let out a disapproving *humph* as I sat down. Hayden's warm hand rested on my shoulder for a beat, sending small butterflies fluttering in my tummy at his touch.

He removed his hand and went to sit back down next to Cara. But he couldn't take his eyes off me. We seemed to share a shy smile at every glance. There was an undeniable feeling being shared between us without words, and it was building feverishly with every second in each other's presence.

As the tables around us gradually filled, a nervous-looking young man in a suit that seemed a size too large for him came over and spoke to Hayden.

"Mister Raynor, the Mayor will present your MVP award first, so don't go anywhere, okay?"

"He a hockey fan?" Hayden asked him, to which the young man shrugged.

"If it gets him votes, then he is."

Then the man scuttled off to find the next person on his hit-list.

Hayden's eyes turned back to meet mine, and I blushed at the raw intention in them, before turning to Jimmy.

"Jimmy, I'm going to the bathroom, okay?"

"Sure, don't be long, though. It's about showtime here."

As I slipped away from the table, I vaguely noticed Cara get up and follow behind me.

In the restroom, I'd just started to check my make-up when Cara came in, set her drink down, and started preening next to me in the mirror. An unsettling feeling rose inside me at her presence.

"So, you snuck your way in, huh?" She said, with a hint of poison in her words as she ran lipstick over her luscious lips. "A kid's teacher rubbing shoulders with all of *us*."

I had no stomach for a fight, so I gathered up my things and replied with a curt, "I guess so."

I turned on my heels, and that was when Cara picked up her glass.

"Nice dress, by the way."

Those were the last words I heard before she turned and splashed her glass of red wine all over me.

I squealed - first in shock, and then horror - at the crimson liquid running down and soaking the beautiful subtle hues of the dress I was wrapped in. Then I looked at Cara in complete disbelief.

"Oops," she giggled, holding her hand up to her mouth.

In an instant, Cara swung her bag over her shoulder, turned away from me, and left me there stunned. I was still open-mouthed and frozen in shock when Andrea Barker walked into the restroom, took a surprised look at me, and exclaimed a sad, "Oh dear."

Hayden

Cara came and sat back down, just as the Mayor came out and the lights dimmed around us.

"Hey, where's Sarah?" I hissed at her.

"I don't know Hayden. I'm not her babysitter. Why don't you call Joyce and ask her?" She said it with all her usual pleasantness.

Mayor Huskins was eating up the applause on the stage before he started his charm offensive, "Now, now. We're not here today for me - as much as that hurts me to say - but for something greater..."

Where was she? I gave Jimmy a puzzled look across the table and he shrugged back. Before I had time to settle, the busy little hummingbird in a suit was on me again. "Okay Mr. Raynor, you ready?"

On cue, the mayor was saying, "Now, usually, the MVP hockey award is handed out elsewhere... I'm not sure exactly where... The backroom of a bar? Stan's Chicken Shack maybe! But tonight, I get the illustrious opportunity to give it out myself to our local star. The captain of the Ice-Hawks, please welcome to the stage, the one and only, Mr. Hayden Raynor!"

A garish spotlight blinded me as I stood and made my way through the thrashing hands toward the stage. Mayor Huskins looked up at me as I approached him and gripped my hand with both of his.

"Hayden, it's an honor to have you here tonight."

"Thank you, Mr. Mayor. Or can I call you Howard?"

"Not even my wife calls me Howard. But looking at the size of you, sure, you can call me pumpkin if you want to."

"Okay. Well, thank you pumpkin."

Laughter rang out as the Mayor stepped away and left

me at the podium holding my award, the thick letters MVP welded together in brass.

"Wow. Thank you for this. I also want to thank Coach Brady, my agent Jimmy Kemp, my teammates, well not all of them, but you know who are, and... And..."

There was an uncomfortable silence in the crowd as I stopped speaking. I knew what I was *supposed* to say. All the usual stuff. Thank everyone, act humble, but not too humble. But I didn't want to say any of those things. My throat was suddenly dry and I cleared it awkwardly.

"I just want to say. All this is great. Getting awards from the Mayor,"—a cheer—"The money,"—A bigger cheer—"The fans. The attention. The excitement out there on the ice... But... I mean. All of it is just a distraction, isn't it?"

Some confused murmurs came from the crowd below me.

"It just fills that void we have. For love. *Real* love, I mean. The kind where you can't sleep. Or think rationally. Or be who you're trying to be. When none of it seems to make sense without them. All of it just leads back to that one thing."

I looked over to our table and Sarah's chair was still empty. All I wanted at that moment was for her to be there so I could go over, take her hand, and walk out of there with her. But she wasn't there, and my words suddenly felt dull and useless in my mouth. "Also... Cara, get out of my house."

There was a confused patter of semi-applause and confusion as I stepped down from the stage and the Mayor went to pick up the pieces, "Hayden Raynor... A lover *and* a fighter...And your MVP!"

Jimmy got to me first. "Hayden, you okay?"

"Where is she, Jimmy?"

"I don't know. She never came back from the restroom."

I glared at Cara and she looked away, avoiding my eyes.

"Where is she Cara?"

The look on my face must have been a sight because, for once, she didn't make any quips or shrug her shoulders. She just squeaked back at me.

"She spilled her drink, made quite a mess of that lovely dress. So, I guess she left?"

It was then that Andrea Barker bumped into Cara's chair as she walked behind her. Andrea's full glass tumbled over Cara's head, leaving her looking like a drowned and astonished rat as she screeched in horror.

"Oh, I'm terribly sorry," Andrea said unconvincingly as she walked away.

The busy little man in the oversized suit then scuttled up to the side of me. "Mr. Raynor, a photo with the Mayor please."

I snarled at him as I thrust the award down on the table, "Not now."

Then I was striding out of the building.

29

STUMBLING

Sarah

I was devastated. The once perfect dress was ruined and my make-up had quickly followed it into oblivion. Once again, I'd tried to step into that other world, finding out very quickly that I wasn't wanted there. That I didn't fit. Humiliated, I'd run straight out of the entrance and away from it all.

All I wanted was to feel was something that wasn't this. *Anything* that wasn't this. That wasn't Hayden or Cara or Mayors or balls or my complete shame.

Outside, the hem of the dress crumpled against the dirty street as I chased down the first cab I saw with tears streaking down my face. Climbing inside and collapsing on the backseat, I groaned out in wild, mad agony. The cab driver gave me an odd look through his rearview mirror, before I found a ridiculous fake smile and gave him my address.

I couldn't face going home to my empty apartment, though. What would I do there? Wallow and relive that fucking moment over and over again in my head? So, when I saw the first green neon lights of a bar, I told the cab driver to turn off.

The night had gotten humid and sticky after the recent rains, and The Jackalope looked lively as we pulled up. Men in denim and leather hung outside in groups under the neon lights, sipping on cold beers and sucking on warm cigarettes, while rock n' roll splashed out onto the pavement with every swing of the faded red door. It was as good a place as any.

An hour ago, I'd attracted admiring looks, but now I only received odd looks as I stepped out of the cab in my disgraced fancy dress. My heels crunched on the gravel as I walked up to the bar and stepped inside the raucous atmosphere of revelry.

People were yelling to each other loudly over the music, dancing wildly in the crowded space, the sound of pool balls echoing from one corner and wild laughter bouncing off the walls from another.

The lone barman was half-drenched in sweat, red-faced, and busy, but he gave me a warm, welcoming smile as I pushed my way up to the bar. *He was cute*, I thought to myself as I smiled back, trying to push everything else from that night out of my mind.

"Hey, so what can I get ya?"

Usually, I would've gone for a cold beer, but that wasn't enough tonight. I didn't want to be slow and introspective. I needed to shake things loose or else end up wallowing in my own misery.

"Tequila. Will you do one with me?" I shouted over the rattle of music.

"Sure!" He replied, grabbing a bottle and setting two long shot glasses down between us.

"What we toasting to?" He asked as he picked up his glass and leaned in closer.

"Um... How about ...Being a big fucking disaster?"

"Done!"

We downed the shots, the tequila hitting my throat and making me gag, before I thankfully sucked on the accompanying slice of lime.

"And now?" The bartender asked. Slamming his glass upside down.

"Another!"

He laughed. "Okay then, but I'll sit this one out."

I pouted back at him, making him roll his eyes.

"Alright, fine! I'm in," he said, and I clapped my hands to show my approval, wondering if that first shot had taken its effect already.

We downed another shot. This one went down easier than the first and I didn't have to dive instantly for the lime, but instead tasted the sharp and sweet oily flavor on my tongue for a moment. The cute bartender stood back and raised an eyebrow at me, waiting for my next request while other faces at the bar leered at him, shaking dollar bills and waiting for their turn.

"Another!" I yelled.

He laughed, but less jovially this time. Looking thoughtful for a second, he leaned over the bar to me.

"How about I make you an El Diablo instead?"

"What's that?" I said, hoping he wasn't making fun of me.

"Tequila, lime, creme de cassis, ginger beer... Seriously, I think you'll love it!"

"Okay!" I yelled back over the music, my limbs already feeling a little looser.

Hockey Heart

He left to fix up my drink, throwing an ice cube over his shoulder and catching it in a glass for my amusement.

"Show off!" I shouted at him, laughing, and he grinned back. I was starting to feel better already. This was way better than that stuffy crowd back at the ball.

A voice to my left rattled in my ear, "Say, don't I know you!"

A craggy-looking man with a black cowboy hat and glassy eyes was looking at me. At least when his eyes didn't lose focus and drift away.

"Nope, I don't think so!" I yelled back.

"Well, let's change that then!"

It made me laugh. He seemed harmless enough, and he was at least eight drinks ahead of me.

"Oh, sorry. I'm married." I bellowed.

"Hi Mary, I'm Max!" he yelled back.

"No, I'm MARRIED."

He stared back at me, not understanding. So I raised my hand and tapped on the ring finger, feeling suddenly sad that there wasn't a ring there, that there never had been, and maybe there never would be.

"No, I'm NOT married!" He called back.

"Hi!" another voice yelled at me from the side.

This one was younger, with nice hair and a coy smile. "Get you a drink?"

The bartender put my pink cocktail down in front of me and then turned to the other faces at the bar, all jostling for attention like a gaggle of baby birds crying out for worms from their momma.

Nice Smile Man looked at the drink and then back at me, "Ha, guess not!"

I leaned in and shouted into his ear so he could hear me.

"I'll have a drink with you, but it's too loud in here!"

He nodded and then pointed his head toward the end of the bar. Hopping off my bar stool, we walked through the thronging crowd to the door at the end and stepped out into the beer garden out back, welcoming the cooler air.

"This place is pretty wild," I told him, breathing a sigh of relief at having escaped the throng of noise and people.

"Yeah, gets that way," he said, smiling bashfully.

He was maybe half a foot taller than me, dressed in a casual black shirt, blue jeans, and black cowboy boots, matching his thick dark hair and brown eyes.

"Jessie," he told me, holding out a hand as if we were in a business meeting.

I don't know why I did it, but I paused for a second before answering him with, "Kensy."

What the hell was that, Sarah? Even if you were going to give him a pretend name, don't make it your best friends.

"Cool." Jessie replied, taking a long sip of his beer and watching me with his vibrant eyes, "Haven't seen you here before. New in town?"

"That's right, came in with the breeze."

Weird Sarah, no one talks like that.

"Ah, like a storm?"

"Could be," I teased, running my finger around the edge of my glass and looking up at him.

Oh God, you're flirting with him... He is sort of hot though... Small, dark, and handsome... And normal, an actual normal person...

"So, what? You ran away from the ball?"

I froze. How could he know that?

"The dress I mean," his eyes pointed to what I was wearing, "It looks like you just came from some kind of ball or something."

"Oh. I guess I just felt a little extravagant tonight," I replied, relieved.

A group of hyped-up girls came whooping past us, their cigarette break over as they went back to the party, knocking my drink from my hand without noticing or stopping.

"Oh, shoot!" Jessie said, as we both looked down at the pink mess around my feet.

I sighed and told him, "I don't want to go back in there."

"Me either," he replied, looking deep into my eyes.

30

THE RING

Hayden

Everything was blurred. I didn't even know what I was doing exactly. All I knew when I pushed my way out of City Hall was that I had to find *her*.

I grabbed my keys from the concierge and headed out to Sarah's home first. Where else would she go? The truth is, I had no idea. But it was the only place I could think to start.

The lights were on as I pulled up outside and jogged up to her door, banging on it with my fist until I heard footsteps approach.

"Who is it?"

"It's me," I said through the door, my heart pounding.

"Um, Sarah's not here."

I sighed painfully. "Yeah. Okay. I get it. Look, I don't know what Cara did tonight, but you have to know that, after you left, I realized the only person I wanted there was you.

Sarah, I don't know what's happening. But for some reason, I can't shake... I think you're the most special person that might ever have come into my life. And yeah, I know how that sounds. And I know I keep messing it up. But I don't want to mess it up anymore. I want to... I just... I just want you.

I can't help it and I can't stop it. I'm either thinking about you or dreaming about you. And yeah, I know you think I'm this big, strong, rich fantasy, but I'm so much more than that. I just have to hide it. All the damn time. If I don't, I'll get eaten alive by all these people in my world. But it never feels like that with you."

I waited for her to speak, the rocks piling up in my stomach. Then the lock turned in the door and it crept open. I looked up at her face and recoiled at the woman in curlers standing in the doorway.

"So, yeah. Like I said, Sarah's not here," Kensy said.

Fuck.

"I need to find her. Please, help me."

"Okay. Well, let's not do this in the street, come inside Hayden."

I followed her inside, my feelings softening at seeing the inside of Sarah's apartment again. I already had already memories tied up in that place. That sofa, the kitchen, her bedroom. She got her phone and held it up to her ear.

"Okay. She's not picking up. What happened exactly?"

"I don't know. Cara maybe did or said something to her. She just disappeared."

"Oh, Cara? Yeah, she gave Sarah the stick when we came over the other night."

"Wait. You came to my place?"

"Uh-huh. Sarah came to tell you she'd come to the ball with you, but then Cara answered and after that, we left pretty sharpish."

"Cara didn't tell me about that. *Of course,* she didn't tell me!"

Kensy stared at me with a sympathetic look. I wasn't used to people looking at me like that and I felt embarrassed by it.

"Look," she said, pondering the situation, "If it was me. Well, I'd either go home and cry it out, or I'd take myself to the nearest bar and try and shake it off. Where else is there to go at this time?"

"Do you know what bar?"

"Any place is as good as any other, I'd say. Probably not somewhere I'd be noticed by anyone I knew, though."

"Somewhere between here and the ball then," I jumped up, ready to leap into action. "You coming?"

Kensy looked at me ruefully. "I want to. I really do. But I think this one you have to do alone, Hayden. Just promise me something."

"Okay. What is it?"

"Really mean it, okay? Sarah's not someone to play with. She's terrified you're going to walk into her life and ruin it. If you want to find her, it has to be real. None of this Hellraiser bullshit."

"Fair. And trust me, that's a promise I can keep."

The first two bars I stopped at were a bust. I was starting to lose hope that I would ever find her as I pulled up to The Jackalope. Would she come here? It looked kind of wild.

The great thing about being my size is that you can see most people in a crowd at a glance. My eyes swung over the bar and she wasn't there. But then, just as I was ready to turn and leave, I saw the door at the back of the bar swing open and I caught the vivid shimmer of a dress I recognized. The one she had been wearing. And there she was. Outside, staring gooey-eyed at some guy. My stomach grumbled with anxiety.

"Hayden Raynor!" someone suddenly yelled at me, drawing looks my way.

"Out my way," I growled at him.

I was there for one thing. *Her.*

As I made my way across the room, the door swung open again. Sarah's head turned casually away from that short guy and her eyes widened in recognition as she glimpsed me. She was so small and beautiful that it made my guts rumble again. Damnit, I could skate out in front of thousands of people, cameras, photographers, hockey bunnies, and superstars, but out here I was nervous. This wasn't a battle of strength and sweat and power. I had all the tools for that. This was about feelings, and I felt woefully under-prepared. *No. You got this Hayden, go get the girl.*

She watched me as I pushed my way through the crowd to her, people all around jostling and grabbing at me. *Hayden Raynor's here! Hey, Hellraiser!*

Forcing my way through the wild-eyed crowd, finally I made it and stood in front of Sarah. I might've been 6' 8" but at that moment I felt tiny in her presence. My mouth opened, but no words came out.

"Hayden?" Her soft words reached me. "What are you doing here?"

I gulped hard, feeling my skin redden, my bravado turning to weakness.

"I came... For you," I managed to say, suddenly overcome with shyness.

She gave me a puzzled look back. I knew I would have to elaborate, but now I was faced with her, I didn't know how to. The voices continued to hum around us, but they felt like they were in a different place entirely. *Hayden, have a drink with me! I love you, Hayden! Hey, sign my beer!*

Back in my first game for the Ice-Hawks, I'd had rocks in my stomach the whole game. All the things I knew how to do were somehow stifled and slow and difficult. I did okay perhaps, but I knew I wasn't there to do "okay". Late into the third period, Coach Brady called a time-out at fifty-seven minutes with the scores at 2-2.

"Hayden, you're out there for the next rush."

He'd looked me straight in the eye, like we were the only two people in that arena of noise, and then told me, "Listen, kid. Block it all out and let everything feel loose. You're over-thinking it, trying too hard. Do what's natural and the rest will come."

Suddenly, I'd felt calm. The fans, the lights, the emotion, the fear in my guts, it was all just noise. At the fifty-ninth minute, their right-winger fumbled a pass, and I was on him like a shot, putting him down on the ice and rolling like a steam train over the blue line. I'd exchanged two quick passes with Solly without even thinking about it, faced up their goaltender, and then the whole stadium had erupted.

Now, stood there in front of Sarah, in the game of a lifetime, I closed my eyes and took a long, deep breath. The bar drifted away, the hands pulling on my sleeve. Whoever that guy with her was. The feeling of impending failure. None of it existed. Only her. Only this.

"Sarah. Since I met you, my world has been a mess. I can't explain it, except that when I'm with you, I don't feel lost anymore. There's no one in this whole world that sees me like you do. It only seems to make sense with you. And without you, it's making me go crazy."

The hands stopped grabbing at me and the voices

around us quietened, except for one who yelled, "Hey! Stop the music!"

Those gorgeous soft eyes that made my chest throb looked up at me as she spoke.

"Hayden. Since you came into my life, I've been losing everything. It scares me that none of this is real. That, even though it's what I want, what's waiting for me at the end is only going to be painful."

My breath beat harder. I couldn't give this up.

"You're not the only one who's scared, Sarah. I'm terrified of this. For me. For Maiden. Every time a woman comes into our lives, everything gets worse."

"Maybe it's just your choice in women, Hayden?" She shot back at me.

I loved it when she looked at me and those small crinkles at the edge of her beautiful eyes made the world feel suddenly soft and light.

"Could be," I smiled back. "But when I'm not with you, I'm thinking of you, and when I'm with you, it's the only time I feel real."

Sarah took a step toward me and, as she did so, I put my hand in my pocket, my fingers finding their way around the edges of the ring. Her ring.

She'd told me about it the first time we met. Even then, when I didn't know what would come next, I'd wanted to get it back to her.

Finding it wasn't hard. I figured she would've used a pawn shop close to either her work or home. Out of the three, the second one had remembered the lady and knew the ring I meant. Two days ago, the day after I'd left her apartment, I'd gone and picked it up.

I tried to block out all the hushed faces that now stood

watching us. The glow of the camera phones. The space between us that I desperately wanted to close.

Sarah put her hand on my shoulder. Her eyes were mesmeric, and I looked fearfully for the answer in them and saw it. And that's right when I fumbled the ring...

Sarah

My heart was racing, and not just because of Hayden stood there pouring his heart out. The tequila was running thick in my blood now and blurring my emotions. The next thing I knew, Hayden was down on one knee and, when he looked up again, in his hands he was holding up a ring between his fingers. There was a gasp around the room. Mine included.

He looked shocked at the reaction around him and began protesting, "Oh, no! No, this isn't *that*..."

My eyes focused in on the ring in his hand, and then my surprise turned to recognition, "Wait, is that..."

He stared at me with those hazel puppy dog eyes as I reached out to it and soft tears rose in my eyes. *My Grandma's ring. It couldn't be.* I looked back at him in astonishment. Watching this huge man on his knees, vulnerable and offering himself, holding the one thing I couldn't imagine.

"Do you really mean it, Hayden?"

His expression was so fragile, yet intense. His words seeming to come from deep within his heart.

"Even on that first terrible date, it was there. I tried to deny it, but I couldn't shake it. Ever since then, I always felt like I had to find my way back to you. I want to find out more than anything, Sarah. If you can give me a chance, I promise I'll give it everything I have. And that's the truth."

I gulped while he waited down on his knee for my answer. And it wasn't just me. The whole bar seemed to suck in the air and were now hushed and waiting anxiously for my response.

Which is right when my stomach turned. Hayden's expression turned to puzzlement as my eyes and cheeks bulged. And then, in that almost perfect moment, I threw up.

31

KNOWING

Sarah

I woke up with my head swimming, feeling like I'd slept in a swamp. My mouth was dry, and I was in an unfamiliar bed.

Groaning, I looked to my left and saw a glass of water and two Advil, placed there for my benefit. Then I groaned even more when I saw what was hanging on the closet. The once fabulous dress. Looking like it had been taken on a ride through hell by a motorcycle gang. The red wine stains, dirt, and bile told the story of how it - and I - had got there. But it didn't say exactly how.

I pulled myself up uneasily, a sharp pain throbbing behind my eyes, and heard the door creak open.

"Good morning. Well... Almost," he said as he casually walked in. *Oh God. I was at Hayden's.*

I could smell the rich aroma of coffee from the mug that his hands were wrapped around. He held it out to me with a smile and I took it suspiciously, desperately trying to recall the night before, and wondering exactly what I was doing there in that bed. As I took the coffee, I noticed with a flutter of delight my grandma's ring on my hand.

"Hayden, did we..." I uttered through my dry throat.

He gulped back at me.

Oh God, had we?

"I put you to bed. That's all." He replied.

I squinted at him, even more suspiciously this time, to make sure he was telling the truth.

"What are these?" I pulled at the huge *USA Hockey* t-shirt that covered me like a blanket and the enormous tartan print pants.

"Well, I couldn't let you sleep in that." His eyes led mine once more toward the dress, now hanging like a tattered mess.

"So. You... Undressed me?"

Hayden coughed and looked away awkwardly. "I tried my best not to look too much."

"Thank you," I replied shyly.

Hayden

It was true. I had tried not to. Tried to keep my eyes from that warm, inviting skin, those soft thighs, the divine stretch of her back. In that moment, my only intention was to help her, though. I loved that I could do that for her.

I'd never got my answer, but at least I was with her. Something about that felt so right. I knew deep down that this was either going to be the start of something or the end. I was in turmoil about which one it would be.

I'd played all my cards. All that was left was for her to show her hand, and then we would know. *Just for once, can this not be temporary but something real?*

Sarah

"So, you wanna grab a shower?" He asked me.

"Do I need one?"

Hayden sniffed the air theatrically and laughed, before I took a sniff at myself.

"Oof. Okay. Point taken."

I paused, still wondering, before I asked him, "Did you mean it?"

He raised his eyebrows back at me.

"I mean, last night. The things you said."

Hayden's demeanor turned shy and nervous. Those beautiful dark eyes, like wide mystical moons, looked back at me, full of mystery, and he nodded bashfully.

"You mean, when I was down on one knee holding up a ring with everyone watching?"

I smiled back at him. It had been quite the look.

"Sarah... I meant every word."

Now, it was my turn to gulp. My eyes fell away from his and traveled down across his strong frame. While I was thankful he hadn't taken advantage of me, a swelling part of me was disappointed. I felt desire rise and prickle my skin, and he saw it in me as our eyes met. That strange feeling between us rippled up again. A thousand words couldn't have said what our eyes did to each other.

I climbed clumsily out of the bed and stood before him, us both admiring each other, our skin wanting to feel the touch of the others. The attraction was wild and undeniable.

"A shower sounds like a good idea," I said softly.

I took his hand and pulled him behind me, leading Hayden with me into the bathroom.

I turned to him and rested my ass against the sink as he

came in closer, his breath short and anxious, matching my own. His eyes were sparkling, showing his every desire. He was only waiting for my permission.

"This time you *can* look while you undress me."

Hayden didn't hesitate. Those huge hands, full of strength and aggression, were as soft and gentle as snow as they slipped to my sides and pulled up my oversized shirt, revealing my soft belly, then the tender curves of my breasts that were held within the black bra I couldn't wait to remove.

Slowly and deliberately, Hayden undressed me, savoring each piece of enticing flesh that made his heart thump. I turned for him and let him unfasten my bra, hearing his sharp breath as his fingers traced along my back, his touch on my skin making me quiver and sharpen with desire.

I reached behind me and took his hands in mine, pushing them down to the waistband of my giant-sized pants and then releasing them, letting him have the satisfaction and indulgence of slipping them down over my hips and my ass.

My skin felt wild and beautiful as he rolled the brushed cotton down my thighs, stepping out as they reached each ankle. His hand wrapped around each of my ankles, as if he was mystified by them, like they were a new and wonderful discovery delivered by the Gods. My own eyes closed in bliss as his palms and outstretched fingers slid slowly back up the meat of my legs, finding their way to the top of my panties. We both gasped in thrilled excitement as he pulled them from my hips and down my body, until they lay around my feet.

His frame dwarfed me again as I sensed him rise behind me. One perfectly sculpted arm reached over me and turned the handle that brought water gushing out from the showerhead. His hands held my arms as we waited for the steam to come and join us, then he held out his hand as if he were asking me to dance. My hand looked tiny as I placed it on top of his outstretched palm and he led my naked body forward into the shower.

I turned to him, letting him see me, wanting his eyes, his hands, his lips, all of him, to have all of me. His eyes traveled hungrily along my naked body, hardly able to blink in case he might miss a second of what was before him.

Unable to resist, I reached out and pulled at where his white t-shirt hung over his belt, Hayden lifting his strong arms for me as I lifted the shirt over his head.

The vision of that ripple of muscles made me softly bite my lip with wild desire. My fingers were almost scared to reach out and touch his chest, as if it couldn't be real and would disappear as soon as I tested it. My fingertips found him with reverence, slowly searching out the hard muscle and soft excitement of his body with fascination. So much to discover, and I'd only just started, as I traced a white stretch of scar tissue across his ribcage and delicately touched it.

Hayden stepped forward, forcing me to move a pace backward into the shower. The hot water gushing over us, the steam engulfing our bodies. I turned my back to him as he reached for the shower gel, lathering it decisively between his hands before his thick fingers met my shoulders, massaging them as they responded and softened with sheer bliss.

His hands ran upward through my hair, those thick fingers finding their way to tenderly massage my scalp and run deep into my hair. As he reached past me for the bath sponge, I was beyond eager for him to take that soapy sponge all over me. All my fantasies were suddenly coming to life, as if he knew exactly what I wanted. I was completely given over to him as he slipped those bubbles over my skin, exploring every part of my body, making me clean for him in the wild heat of the steam that enveloped us.

I felt him leave me and turned to see Hayden holding out a towel for me. Stepped out, I let him cover me in it, patting down and drying the same skin that he had been blissfully teasing and caressing only moments ago.

Turning to Hayden, my hands rose and rested on his shoulders, and the look in our eyes said everything. Then, in one swift and divine movement, he scooped me up off my feet and carried me effortlessly back into the bedroom.

Throwing me down onto the bed, I felt wild for him.

"Hayden, I think you might make me crazy."

He turned to me with a wicked glint in his eye and ran his thick thumb over my lips.

"Hush now. Those lips aren't for words. Right now they've got other work to do."

I giggled at his brazen confidence, but I wasn't about to argue either as I rolled on top of his huge frame and let my mouth run kisses down his chest, heading lower and lower under the rich cotton sheets.

Sarah

I wanted to stay in that blissful state forever, wrapped up gleefully in the sheets with each other, exploring every sweet indulgence we could imagine. If only I could.

"I have to go."

"I know." He sighed back, as if just the thought of it made him ache.

"I really don't want to, though."

"Let me drive you."

"Sure, I'd like that."

Outside, we sat in his car for a beautiful moment, both of us smiling shyly. Then our lips found each other again, and it all faded away. He wasn't a hockey player or a fantasy anymore. He was just Hayden and, right now, he was mine. For the first time since I came back to Merryville, I wasn't a teacher or a confused mess. I was his. And that mountain of a man had let his heart soften until it had melted into mine.

Love had leveled us. Now, it might just heal us.

32

BALL BABE?

Cara

To hell with this. It was time for me to leave. Not just Merryville, but perhaps a part of me behind too.

I might tell you that you've got the wrong idea of me, that we all do terrible things every day, and that you're no different. But that's not entirely true. Yes, I do terrible things, but the fact is, I enjoyed doing them. That, at least, I can admit to. Can you?

And why change when you always get what you want? The thing was, though, I wasn't so sure I did get what I wanted anymore. Or even what it was I wanted in the first place.

I was shockingly brilliant at being a thorn in people's lives, but that was proving to be a lot less fun than it used to be. Because, like I already said (keep up, will you?), I always got what I wanted.

But Solly, Hayden, somehow all of them were now getting everything they wanted. And maybe, if I really care to think about it, this time I hadn't.

I mean, Hayden and that goofy teacher, what the heck was up with that? Those gooey eyes they were giving each other all night at the ball were beyond nauseating. Then I'd heard them stumbling in that night like lovestruck teenagers, despite my best efforts.

On the bright side, she would be better for Maiden than I ever would be, and that kid deserved the world. One I couldn't give him. Too selfish. Too unmotherly. I can admit that too. But don't think I'm so cold that I don't care.

And look, it's not that I didn't want Hay to be happy either, but not if I wasn't. And I hadn't been for a while. Happy, that is. So, sure, maybe I made things a little hard for him sometimes, and you can judge me all you want for that. But he's a goddamn hockey player! He could handle a little rough and tumble, couldn't he?

Then, of course, there was that whole drama with Solly. Who I'd helped out, but only after I'd helped myself to him first. Now he'd gone crawling back cowering to that neurotic and jealous wife of his. All of it made me feel like I really wasn't on my game anymore.

But, if they can change, I can too. Don't get me wrong. I'm not softening up. When one door closes, another opens, and there's a new door already opening on the West Coast for me. I'm about to board for LAX, where Logan Beattie will be picking me up. Yes, THE Logan Beattie. What's the baseball equivalent of a puck bunny anyway? A ball babe? Well, whatever it was, I was about to find out. It was time to move on to something new.

Maybe you'll think I'm delusional (*I really couldn't care less by the way*), but in a funny way, I'd helped all this come about, hadn't I? So give credit where it's due. Everyone is happy because of *me*. Queen Cara. So, I'll gracefully accept your applause right now.

Perhaps we'll see each other again, when you're handing me my coffee, packing my groceries, trying to clean my windscreen at traffic lights, or whatever it is you regular people do. Hey, we can't all be me.

33

COULD THIS BE?

Sarah

"...After that heavy hit, it looks like Hayden and Sampson are about to renew their rivalry from last season, get ready for some heavy hitting from these two heavyweights... Oh, wait! What's happening here? Hayden Raynor, hockey's bad boy, refuses to drop the gloves! For the third game running, the Hellraiser has declined the invitation! I can't believe what I'm seeing... The crowd are on their feet howling as Raynor turns and points a glove toward someone in the crowd...

What a change we've seen in this player. His most goals and assists in a season since he joined the team. He looks sharp, focused, not the brawler we all know!"

Hayden turned off the game highlights and sunk his head under the bubbles of the hot tub, rising back up through the steam like my own personal fantasy come to life. Six months later, and I still had those giddy feelings about him.

"More Champagne, my lady?"

"Sure. I still can't believe you haven't seen The Holiday!"

"Me either. Let's do it."

I curled up to him in the tub, my head on his wet chest as his heavy arm wrapped its way around me and pulled me closer to him. I felt safe and, dare I even say it, happy, as I listened to his thumping heart beneath his wide chest.

Hayden hit the remote and the movie started on the flatscreen. Then he pressed a button and the hot-tub roared into life. We both giggled as the bubbles rippled across our naked skin.

So much had changed. After years of feeling stuck, suddenly everything was new and vibrant. It just goes to prove that wherever you are, whoever you are, there's always the hope that love can change everything in an instant. Even when you've given up.

Of course, it had helped that Cara was now off sinking her talons into someone else, and seemed much less interested in riling Haydon up now. She still called to talk to Maiden though, who told us "Mom's a *cleat chaser* now," after their last chat.

That little guy was doing great, too. After we got him some extra help at school, he was happy and making friends. Which in turn made Haydon happy too. I mean, he hadn't hit anyone in months. He was still going to his therapy though, even though he didn't have to anymore. Dana was helping him unpack his past, and although it wasn't easy, we were working on it, and I could see the change in him already. Oh, and then there was Kensy! But that's a whole other story to be told…

"I like you without the beard, Hay."

"Well, *someone* once told me I had a crap beard."

"Did they now? Well, I definitely prefer the sexy dad stubble, especially feeling it graze across my thighs."

Hayden looked at me with those dark eyes, our chemistry in motion.

"Hey, we going out with Dan and Kensy tonight, right?"

Hayden laughed, "The odd couple. I like those two together."

"Me too. Let's take my car this time."

"Toto? I can barely get my legs in that fucking thing. Honestly, we could've got you any other car."

"I like watching you trying to get out of her," I laughed at him.

"Sarah?" He asked, softly.

"Hayden?"

"I really like this."

"I really like this too."

The End.

Hayden, Sarah, Kensy, and Cara will return later in the 'Skates and Sparks' series.

THANK YOU!

Thank you SO much for reading Hockey Heart! I really hope you enjoyed it as much as I did writing it. As a small favor, if you enjoyed the story and could take a moment to leave me a review on the kindle store, that would absolutely make my day!

Y'know, it's a strange fuzzy feeling when you finish a book, mixed with a hint of sadness that it's all over. Well, it doesn't have to be just yet!

You can get free chapters, stories, exclusive news and offers on new releases, and much more by signing up to my newsletter. Just go to the link below for some sweet bi-monthly romance action delivered straight to your inbox.

www.katewilderbooks.com

The next book in the 'Skates and Sparks' series is also just around the corner! Turn the page now for a sneak-peak of *Breakaway Heart*...

Thank you so much, I can't wait to see you again soon!

Thank you!

xx K. Wilder

THE 'SKATES AND SPARKS' SERIES

Breakaway Heart

AN OPPOSITES ATTRACT HOCKEY ROMANCE

KATE WILDER

BREAKAWAY HEART

Two weeks off from the world in absolute paradise and I'm eating ice cream in bed with the blinds down and watching Love Villa. Is this who I am?

Lucy Heaton is on her first vacation in three years. A blissful all-inclusive luxury two-week break away from work and guys. *Especially* guys.

Meanwhile, star winger of the Ice-Hawks, Randall Jackson, is spending his summer break showcasing the absolute worst side of himself on the hit celeb dating show, Love Villa. Lucy and America can't look away from the disaster-class unfolding on their screens. And the worst thing? Randall has absolutely no idea his behavior is making him enemy number one outside of the villa.

When Randall is shocked to be voted out as the public's least-liked Villa character - and even more shocked at the reception he gets on the outside - he goes into hiding in a private retreat. Lucy's break away is about to take a wild turn when, in the quiet village near her resort, she runs into the nightmare she did not ask for.

Now Randall wants her to help him be a better person, but is there any saving 'the muggiest man on TV' who thinks love is for losers?

The rulebook just got thrown out in Kate Wilder's sparkling new rom-com, Breakaway Heart.

COMING - Spring 2025

Printed in Great Britain
by Amazon